NINE MONTHS

Isabella

by Maggie Wells

E

EPIC
Press

Isabella
Nine Months: Book #4

Written by Maggie Wells

Copyright © 2016 by Abdo Consulting Group, Inc.

Published by EPIC Press™
PO Box 398166
Minneapolis, MN 55439

Cover design by Candice Keimig
Images for cover art obtained from iStockPhoto.com
Edited by Lisa Owens

LIBRARY OF CONGRESS CATALOGING-IN-PUBLICATION DATA

Wells, Maggie.
Isabella / Maggie Wells.
p. cm. — (Nine months; #4)
Summary: Isabella and Carlos live in St. Louis, Missouri. While finishing their senior
year in high school, they decide to have a baby together and get married. When
Carlos joins the military and tragedy strikes, Isabella is devastated. A year later, she is
reunited with Pete, a boy she thinks is her second chance at love. But he could have
a dark side that puts Isabella and her baby's safety in danger.
ISBN 978-1-68076-193-1 (hardcover)
1. Teenagers—Sexual behavior—Fiction. 2. Teenage pregnancy—Fiction. 3. High
schools—Fiction. 4. Sex—Fiction. 5. Young adult fiction. I. Title.
[Fic]—dc23
2015949413

EPIC
Press

EPICPRESS.COM

To Jane Anne Staw,
who taught me to keep going when I get stuck

One

IZZY

CARLOS AND ISABELLA HAD NEVER BEEN OUTSIDE OF St. Louis before. On the bus ride to New Orleans, his gaze was fixed on the passing countryside. Izzy was more interested in the people inside the bus; she was curious about their lives, where they were from and where they were going. Carlos followed the bus's route on his Google maps app and called out landmarks. With each town they passed, Carlos made note of the name and looked it up on Wikipedia and read a factoid aloud. On her frequent trips to the bathroom, Izzy eavesdropped on conversations and whispered to Carlos what she had heard. Together they made up stories about the people and the places, weaving the plot of an adventure film.

"Festus, Missouri," Carlos read. "They could not decide what to name the city so they agreed to shoot a gun at a Bible and whatever proper name was closest to the last page the bullet penetrated would be chosen. The first proper name encountered was that of Porcius Festus, the governor of Judea around sixty AD. Acts twenty-four, verse twenty-seven."

"Two rows ahead, on the right," whispered Izzy. "See the older gentleman—in his mid-sixties, maybe, wearing a leather jacket with a felt hat and glasses, reading a newspaper and nodding off. He is a Professor of history at University of Missouri. He's going to Festus for the annual Bible-shooting re-enactment."

Carlos and Izzy doubled over in a fit of giggles.

A woman sitting three rows ahead of them turned around and glared.

"Oh God," Izzy said, grabbing her belly. "I need to pee again."

//

Carlos and Izzy had met during their sophomore year of high school. Izzy's parents had divorced when she was fifteen and her mom had moved into a townhouse on the far west side of town where Izzy knew no one. She felt awkward and shy in high school. All of the other girls had established cliques and nobody seemed particularly interested in including her. Her only friend was Mr. Pickles, her obese Siamese cat.

Izzy spent her free periods in the library, helping Mrs. Jeffers shelve books. That's where she was when Carlos came in one day to return an overdue book. For some reason he came over to talk to her. She was immediately smitten. It wasn't anything he said—it was the way he listened to her. Like he was really interested in knowing everything about her. He called her the next day and they had been inseparable ever since. Carlos always knew what to say to help her overcome her shyness. He thought she was beautiful, even with her impossibly frizzy hair and crooked front tooth.

///

When she returned to her seat, Carlos was engrossed in his phone and didn't even look up.

"New Madrid, Missouri," Carlos read. "Originally a Spanish territory, the governor welcomed settlers from the United States but required them to become citizens of Spain. It was sold to France in eighteen hundred and then re-sold to the U.S. in eighteen hundred and three as part of the Louisiana Purchase."

"Check out the tall bald man in a fur-lined parka in the row behind us," whispered Izzy. "Why is he wearing a parka in June?"

"What does that have to do with New Madrid?" Carlos asked.

"Um," Izzy said. "He's not from here. He's from somewhere in the Southern Hemisphere where it's cold in June. Argentina! He's from Argentina. He thinks he's in Spain and he got New Madrid confused with Madrid. Won't he be surprised?" She laughed and that bitchy woman from three rows up whipped her head around again.

"What is her problem?" Izzy muttered. She tilted her seat back and closed her eyes.

She thought back to the previous Christmas. Izzy loved Christmastime in St. Louis. The streets were bathed in the glow of millions of tiny white lights. Izzy remembered sitting on the plush carpet floor of her bedroom, wrapping Christmas presents for her cousins' kids. Most of the gifts she had made herself: knitting hats, scarves, and mittens in everyone's favorite colors. She had saved wrapping Carlos's gift for last—a *G-shock Gravitymaster* military-style watch. It was designed to withstand the shock of three forces: gravitational, centrifugal, and vibrational, and it connected to satellites around the world for split-second precision timing. She smiled with the knowledge that he would never again have an excuse to be late.

She opened her left eye a crack. *Yep, he's wearing it*, she thought with a smile. For Christmas, Carlos had surprised her with a ring.

Izzy was sitting by the fire rubbing Mr. Pickles's tummy and humming along to Frank Sinatra Christmas songs playing from her iPod when her phone vibrated. It was a text from Carlos.

I need to talk to you

Carlos was always doing stuff like this, Izzy thought. There was always something urgent he needed to talk to her about. Like the time she had rushed to his house in response to an urgent text. A baby bird had fallen out of its nest and Carlos needed her to drive him to the wildlife rescue center. The bird died before they even got into the car and Carlos was inconsolable. And then there was the time he said he had something important to show her and it turned out to be a Little League team photo from fourth grade that someone had posted on Facebook.

"What's so urgent?" Izzy asked when Carlos arrived. Carlos was tall and wiry with curly brown hair and big brown eyes. He shifted nervously from foot to foot.

"I wanted to give you your gift early," Carlos said. "I couldn't wait."

He dug into his coat pocket and pulled out a small package. "Open it," he said.

Izzy ripped off the wrapping paper and opened the package. Inside was a velvet ring box with a quarter-carat diamond in a white gold setting. It was the most beautiful ring she'd ever seen. *Yes, I'll marry you. Yes, yes, yes!* She smiled at the memory.

Two

CARLOS

CARLOS NOTICED IZZY TWISTING HER RING ON HER finger. He had always planned to join the Marines right out of high school and wanted to get married before he was deployed. He was so happy that he had picked out a ring that she loved. He closed his eyes and smiled at the memory of shopping for the ring. He had had no idea what he was doing.

He had stood at the counter in Kay Jewelers in the South County Center Mall for what seemed like forever, trying to decide which one to buy. He hadn't realized how many different choices there were. *What if I pick the wrong one?* he'd thought. *What if she doesn't like it?* Christmas music had blared from the speakers hung from the ceiling. God, he hated Christmas music!

"Can I help you, sir?" Her nametag read Francesca.

"I'm looking for a ring for my girlfriend," Carlos said.

"Tell me about her," Francesca said. "What is her style?"

Style? Carlos thought. *What is her style?*

"What's her name?" Francesca asked.

"Isabella," Carlos said. "She has frizzy hair and big green eyes."

"Frizzy?" Francesca asked. "You mean curly or wavy?"

"No," Carlos replied. "It's just frizzy. She hates it but I don't see what the big deal is."

"Isabella is a pretty name," Francesca said, recovering. "Is she a girly girl? What does she like to do? Does she wear dresses or jeans most of the time?"

"She likes to knit," Carlos said. "And draw. She's an artist, kind of."

"Oh, creative," Francesca said. "That gives me an idea. How much do you want to spend?"

"How much are they?" Carlos asked.

"Engagement rings start at four hundred ninety-nine and go up to fifty thousand," Francesca said.

Fifty thousand dollars! Carlos thought. He started to feel sick. *Who pays that much money for a ring? In St. Louis?*

"How many fifty-thousand-dollar rings do you sell in a month?" Carlos asked.

Francesca laughed. "You'd be surprised," she said.

"What can I get for around seven-fifty?" Carlos asked.

"Since Isabella is a creative type, I'd recommend . . . " Francesca scanned the display case and selected a ring, which she then laid gently onto a white velvet pillow. "This one is pretty—a classic round diamond enhanced by more diamonds lining the band. Twists of ten-karat white gold winding around the center add a little extra style. It is very delicate, very feminine. What do you think?" she asked.

"It's beautiful," Carlos. "How much is it?"

Francesca turned the tag over. "Seven hundred ninety-nine," she said.

"I'll take it!" Carlos said.

"What size is she?" Francesca said.

"Size?" Carlos asked. "They come in different sizes?"

"Her ring size," Francesca said. "Everybody's hands are different."

Carlos closed his eyes and imagined Izzy's hand. What kind of fingers did Izzy have? He imagined her knitting, winding the strand of yarn around the end of the needle. She had small hands and her fingers were, what? . . . not pudgy exactly. He remembered looking at Francesca's hands. She had long, slender fingers. He glanced around at the other holiday shoppers and spotted a short, stocky woman who was fingering a pearl necklace.

"I think the same size as that lady," he said, and gestured. "What size would that be?"

"Let's try a seven," Francesca said. "You can always bring it back to have it re-sized."

Francesca rang up the sale. Carlos watched as she boxed up the ring, wrapping it in gold foil and topping it with a red-and-gold striped bow. She placed the package into a small cellophane bag with handles.

"Merry Christmas!" Francesca said as she handed the bag to Carlos. "She'll love it. I promise."

///

They had a quickie wedding the week after graduation and now they were on their way to New Orleans for their honeymoon. Since they had stopped using condoms shortly after Christmas, Izzy was already six weeks pregnant. All she wanted in life was to create a family with Carlos, a large, happy, loving family—one completely different than her own. They were both excited about the pregnancy, but Izzy was terrified at the prospect of facing the next eight months alone while Carlos went off to Afghanistan.

Izzy stroked her belly.

"Are you feeling okay?" Carlos asked.

Izzy opened her eyes. She leaned over and kissed his neck. "I'm fine. I'm just a little sad that you'll be leaving in a week and I'll be all alone."

"You won't be alone," Carlos said. "You'll have my mom."

They had decided that Izzy would stay with Carlos's family while he was away.

"But I barely know your parents!" Izzy cried.

"My parents love you. You know that." Carlos put his arm around Izzy and squeezed her. "You know you can't stay with your mom," Carlos said. "That's a bad situation." He tipped his hand to his mouth in the universal gesture for an alcoholic.

Izzy frowned.

Three

IZZY

Izzy's mom had erupted in anger when Izzy told her about the wedding plans.

"Over my dead body!" Dotty said. "Are you pregnant?"

"Of course not!" Izzy said.

"Then why are you rushing?" Dotty asked.

"We're not rushing," Izzy said. "We have been together for two years. Geez, I thought you'd be happy for me."

"I thought you were planning to go to community college," Dotty said.

"I can still do that," Izzy protested. "Carlos will be off fighting jihadists in the Middle East while I'm in college."

"Then why get married?" Dotty asked.

"Why does anyone get married?" Izzy asked. "Why did you and Daddy get married? You weren't much older than I am now, were you?"

"You know that I was pregnant," Dotty said. "I was damaged goods. I dropped out of college to marry your dad and he was in the Navy. When you were a baby, he was always at sea. He even missed your birth. You don't want to be alone like that. You should stay single and keep your options open."

"I don't understand—why can't you be happy for me?" Izzy cried.

Dotty didn't answer. She just poured herself another glass of Scotch.

//

The bus driver announced a one-hour rest stop in Memphis and the passengers filed off. Carlos and Izzy stood on the steaming pavement with thirty other passengers.

"Memphis," Carlos said. "I've always wanted to see Memphis. Want to stay here overnight?"

"What about New Orleans?" Izzy asked.

"We'll catch a bus in the morning," Carlos said. "I want to see Graceland. Are you up for it?"

"What about our bags?" Izzy asked. "What about our Airbnb reservation in New Orleans?" This was a side of Carlos that she didn't recognize. They always had made a plan and stuck to it. It scared her to think that he would abandon their plans so easily.

"I'll text the guy in New Orleans, don't worry," Carlos said over his shoulder as he walked away, looking for the bus driver.

Izzy suddenly felt very alone and very far from home. Something seemed different about being married and she did not like the feeling. Was she imagining it or had Carlos been nicer and more considerate before they were married? Would he have just changed plans without asking her before? He had just left his pregnant wife standing in the parking lot of a bus station in Memphis. *Oh God, I have to pee again,* she thought. She headed into the station and found the ladies room.

When she returned to the waiting room, Izzy saw Carlos pacing back and forth in the parking lot. He had retrieved their luggage.

Carlos saw Izzy and rushed to her. "Where have you been?" he cried. "I couldn't find you."

"I had to pee," Izzy said.

Carlos laughed and embraced her. "I was worried that you got lost. I was so afraid."

Izzy felt bad for doubting his feelings for her.

"So here's the plan," Carlos said. "If you're okay with it, I mean. I found a place to stay, and its near downtown. We can take a cab there, drop our stuff and cab it down to Graceland for the afternoon tour. We still have time. Or, we can get back on the bus for another ten hours. What do you say?"

"That's easy—Graceland," Izzy said. "Let's do it!"

"That's my girl!" Carlos hailed a cab and loaded their bags into the trunk. He read the address of the rental to the driver.

"Are we staying with anyone or will it just be us?" Izzy asked.

"They are renting us a room. Names are Kathy and Jon —they are newlyweds, just like us," Carlos said. "I told them we are on our honeymoon and Kathy said she is really excited to meet you. They asked if we'd like to have dinner with them tonight."

"Really?" Izzy said. "But we're complete strangers. Does that seem a little weird to you?"

"You're going to have to start learning how to make new friends," Carlos said. "I'm not always going to be here."

//

When they arrived at the house, the key was tucked under the mat along with a note.

Hi, Izzy and Carlos. Welcome to Memphis! The dogs in the back yard are Sadie and Max and they are friendly. Please don't let them in the house. Your room is the blue one behind the bathroom. We've left clean towels for you. We'll be home from work by six. Enjoy your visit to Graceland.

Kathy & Jon.

Carlos opened the door and Izzy walked tentatively down the hallway until she found the bathroom. The "blue room" was a screened-in porch furnished with a nasty-looking brown futon sofa and not much else. The dogs were jumping on the screen door, barking.

"Down!" Carlos commanded. The dogs quieted.

"Is there only one bathroom?" Izzy asked.

"Look, it's only forty bucks," Carlos said. "We are here one night and we'll be on the bus to New Orleans tomorrow."

Izzy gave him a skeptical look but dropped her

bag next to the futon and followed Carlos back to the street where the cab driver was waiting.

"Graceland!" Carlos commanded. "Buckle up, sweetie," he said to Izzy.

///

Izzy had never been a big Elvis fan but there was something about touring Graceland that captivated her. At Graceland, Elvis came to life for her; she saw him in a vulnerable human way and she felt a deep empathy for him and his family. Carlos paused in each room of the house and stared at each bit of memorabilia, apparently needing to memorize every detail. Izzy's approach to museums of any kind was to take a quick survey of a room, zero in on the one, most interesting item, study it for a minute and then move on to the next room. She could tour the entire St. Louis Art Museum in under an hour. Izzy found herself way ahead of Carlos within minutes. After touring the main house, the trophy building, and the racquetball building, she found a seat in the meditation garden and waited for Carlos to find her.

//

"There you are!" Carlos said. "Isn't this the best? Did you love it?"

"Very touching, actually," Izzy said.

"Did you see the jungle room?" Carlos asked, excitedly.

"Yes, honey," Izzy said. "Can we go now?"

"Yeah, they're closing," Carlos said. "We have to go. What do you say we take a walk down Beale Street while we're here? Who knows when we'll be back in Memphis, right?"

"Beale Street?" Izzy asked.

"Home of the blues, baby!" Carlos said. "Louis Armstrong, Muddy Waters, B.B. King?"

"I don't know who those people are," Izzy said. *I'm not sure I know who you are either,* she said to herself. Carlos had never once, in the two years she had known him, mentioned Memphis, Elvis, or the blues.

"Let's check it out," Carlos said. "Are you okay? You seem a little cranky."

"I'm a little tired," Izzy said. "But I'm okay. Let's go to Beale Street. Yay."

///

Beale Street was dead. Izzy didn't see what the attraction was for Carlos, or for anybody else for that matter. It had a few bars, cheesy restaurants, and some souvenir shops. The surrounding neighborhood looked run down and sketchy. *The Old North neighborhood of St. Louis is better than this,* she thought.

"Izzy, you really don't seem to be enjoying yourself," Carlos said. They had found a table at Miss Polly's and had ordered chicken and waffles. "This is our honeymoon, baby. What's up with you?"

"Maybe it's just my hormones," Izzy said. "It's

been a long day. Have you heard from your mom?" Izzy was hoping to change the conversation to avoid a fight. *Maybe it is just my hormones.* She wanted to avoid criticizing Carlos. She thought about Carlos's parents, Ricardo and Gilda, who never got cross with each other. At least she had never heard an argument between them.

The waitress delivered their food and Izzy suddenly remembered. "Aren't Kathy and Jon expecting us for dinner?"

"Do you really want to have dinner with two complete strangers?" Carlos asked.

"Thank you, no," Izzy said. "I thought you did."

"No, I was just trying to make you feel welcome here," Carlos said. "I told them we were going to Beale Street for dinner. They are chill."

Izzy picked at her waffle for a few minutes.

"Carlos," she said, putting her fork down. "We're married now."

"Yes," he said.

"I feel like you're not telling me anything until

after you've already decided on it," Izzy said. "I want to be in on the decision."

"What decision?" he asked.

"All of them," she said. "Like tomorrow. What's the plan for tomorrow?"

"We'll catch the first bus to New Orleans, right?" he asked.

"When is the first bus?" she asked.

"There's only one bus," Carlos said. "It leaves at nine-thirty."

"And then what?" she asked.

"We get to New Orleans at eight-thirty tomorrow night," he said. "I booked us an Airbnb near the French Quarter, remember? We have three days in New Orleans and I promise, when we're there, we'll do whatever you want to do. You can make all the decisions. I'm sorry about Memphis. I guess I got a little carried away. I've always wanted to come here. It was too good to pass up."

"If you had asked me, I would have agreed," Izzy said.

"Well, then we're good, right?" Carlos asked.

"I just want to be asked," she said. "I want to be in on the planning."

The sun was setting and Beale Street was starting to come to life. Neon lights blinked on and the sounds of guitars and saxophones floated out from open doors. Police officers were putting up barricades on either end of the street as crowds started to amass.

"Why don't we hang out and listen to some music," Carlos asked. He cleared their table and deposited their trays in the trash.

"I love you, Izzy," Carlos whispered in her ear as he took her arm and helped her up.

"I love you, too," she said and kissed him.

They stood outside of B.B. King's and swayed to the music, her back to him, his arms embracing her. Izzy's fears subsided and for the moment, she felt safe in his arms.

//

They arrived back at Kathy's house around ten and the place was dark.

"Oh, shit," Carlos said. "I hope we don't wake them up."

Sure enough, as Carlos turned the key in the lock, the dogs rushed the door, barking furiously. A light came on inside the house and Jon appeared at the door.

"Sorry, man," Carlos said. "We didn't mean to wake you."

"We're new to renting out the porch," Jon said. "We thought you'd be back earlier."

"Sorry, man," Carlos said again. He and Izzy tiptoed down the hall.

"Do me a favor," Jon called out in a loud whisper. "Don't flush the toilet tonight and don't use the shower until after seven in the morning. I don't want you to wake up Kathy."

Izzy quietly shut the door to the porch room. "Don't flush?" she whispered. "Seriously?"

"I promise not to do number two if you do," Carlos whispered back.

Izzy laughed and Carlos shushed her. "Quiet!" he said. "We don't want to wake up Kathy!"

"God forbid," Izzy said.

They undressed in silence and climbed under the blankets. The futon was lumpy and smelled like a dog bed.

"Carlos?" Izzy whispered. "Are you awake?"

"Yes," he whispered back.

"Is this our wedding night?" She felt Carlos's body convulse with repressed giggles. "I'll always remember it," she said.

"It's just as you've always dreamed, right?" Carlos said.

"I love you," Izzy said. "It's never boring, with you."

"Boring?" Carlos said. "That's a pretty low bar you have set for me. I promise it will never be boring. I want to take you to the moon."

Carlos stripped off her nighty and they made love, very, very quietly.

Four

IZZY

IZZY AND CARLOS ARRIVED IN NEW ORLEANS ON SUNDAY night and took a cab from the bus station to the loft they had rented. Keely, their host, answered the door.

"Hi, y'all!" Keely said, "Y'all must be tired. Let me show you to your room." They followed her across the hall and into a large loft space that was warmly furnished in deep velvet and crystal chandeliers.

"Wow!" Izzy said. "This is beautiful!"

"Thanks," Keely said. "It's totally private with your own bath, a little kitchenette, and a balcony.

Make sure you lock up all the windows at night. You might be tempted to sleep with the windows open but we had a little cat-burglar incident. Don't get me wrong, this neighborhood is perfectly safe, just don't walk around the streets after dark. You should always take a cab."

Carlos took Izzy's bag from her and stashed it along with his in the closet.

"Y'all got big plans for your visit?" Keely asked. "My husband, Judah, is a professional tour guide—French Quarter, cemeteries, Ninth Ward, ghost tours, you name it, he can take you there."

"That would be awesome!" Carlos said. "Can we book him for tomorrow?"

"Sure," Keely said. "I'll tell him to meet you for breakfast at the Coffee Pot around the corner on St. Peter. Is eight-thirty okay with you?"

Carlos shut the door behind Keely. "I did it again, didn't I?" he asked.

"Kind of," Izzy said. "I thought we were going to do whatever *I* wanted."

"We are," Carlos said. "I promise. You tell Judah what you want to see. I just figured it would help to have somebody show us around."

Izzy walked into Carlos's arms. "You are right, of course," she said.

"Do you want to check out Bourbon Street?" he asked.

"Isn't it a little late?" she asked.

Carlos walked over to the window and opened the French doors onto the balcony. There was a wrought-iron table with two chairs overlooking an interior courtyard that was fragrant with the Bougainvillea that was climbing the brick walls. A fountain gurgled in the middle of the courtyard. Off in the distance they could hear strains of jazz music.

"Baby, we're not in St. Louis anymore," Carlos said. "This town stays open all night. Let's go. Please?"

//

The cab driver dropped them off at the end of Bourbon Street and they waded into the crowd of drunken revelers.

"New Orleans, yeah!" Carlos cried.

Izzy had never seen him happier and she tried hard to share his enthusiasm. She looked skyward to scan the pretty buildings draped in delicate wrought-iron railings. She breathed in deeply the smells of history and decay. She was starting to enjoy herself when Carlos abruptly said, "Wait here. I want to get a Hurricane," he said. He strode off in the direction of Pat O'Brien's.

"Don't leave me alone!" Izzy cried. She ran after Carlos, threading her way through the raucous crowd.

"Show us your tits!" someone shouted.

Izzy looked up to see girls of all ages, some even younger than she, clustered like crows, perched on the balconies overhanging the street. She spun slowly around in the middle of the street, the cacophony of blues and jazz and zydeco bands clashing and colliding in her head. The neon lights sliced through the humid night air that weighed her down like a thermal blanket. The crowd crushed her on all sides and she fought to breathe. She felt hands groping at her blouse.

Izzy started to panic. Then she saw Carlos a few feet in front of her and she fought through the crowd to grab at his shirt. He stopped and swung around abruptly to face her. It wasn't Carlos!

"I'm so sorry!" Izzy said. "I thought you were my husband."

"Are you lost, pretty lady?" the man asked. He pulled her to him and draped his arm heavily over her shoulder, grabbing her breast hard.

"Let me go!" Izzy cried. She pushed him with all her strength and he staggered backwards. Losing his balance on the uneven cobblestones, he fell backwards into the crowd. Someone screamed and Izzy pulled away, searching frantically for Carlos. She saw him a few yards in front of her, scanning the crowd. She ran over to him.

"Hey, there you are," Carlos said. He was holding a plastic cup. "They didn't even card me!"

"Don't leave me like that!" Izzy screamed. "I was scared—I couldn't find you."

"What's the matter?" Carlos asked. "What happened?"

Izzy didn't want to tell Carlos about the other man; she was afraid he might start a fight.

"I got lost in the crowd," she said. She started to cry.

"Let's get out of this mob and find a place to sit down," Carlos said.

Izzy clutched Carlos's arm as they walked east on Bourbon Street, away from the bars, the crowd dissipating and the noise subsiding behind them. "Much better," Carlos said. They turned right on Toulouse Street and spotted Molly's Irish Pub. "This looks quiet, let's try this."

They found a table near a window that opened onto Toulouse. Carlos reached across the table and took Izzy's hands in his.

"We're having fun now, right?" Carlos asked. He sipped from his cup through a straw. "You're okay now?"

Izzy smiled, hoping she looked sincere. The terror she had felt a few minutes before was fresh in her mind. Why had he left her standing alone on Bourbon Street? Why had he left her alone at the Memphis bus station? She fiddled with her wedding ring with the thumb of her left hand. Marriage was a lot different than what she had thought. It's a terrifying feeling to recognize that your partner could lead you blindly and enthusiastically into a dangerous situation that he wasn't prepared to control. She suddenly realized that Carlos was just a big, loveable kid. He wasn't ready to be a husband and a father. She felt so much older than him at that moment. But, maybe his stint in the Marines would change him—mature him. Maybe he'd come back from war a man.

///

In the morning, they met Judah for breakfast at the appointed time.

"What would y'all like to see while you're here?" Judah asked.

Carlos looked at Izzy. "Whatever you want, baby."

Izzy pulled out her guidebook. "I've always heard about the cemeteries and of course the Ninth Ward. What is the most popular?"

"Those are definitely in the top five," Judah said. "Also the Garden District for brunch and then one evening you should check out the music scene on Magazine, or catch a classic movie at the Prytania Theater. And there's always the ghost tour. It's a little hokey but you get to see other parts of the French Quarter, off the beaten path. During the day, you should check out the antique shops on Royal Street if you are into that kind of thing. Don't miss the French Market to get some beignets and chicory coffee. And of course there's always Brennan's and Commander's Palace for dinner if you have that kind of green."

Izzy unfolded a map. "Can you highlight every-thing you said?" she asked.

Judah took the highlighter from Izzy and circled all the points of interest.

When he had finished, he asked, "Where do we start?"

Izzy looked at Carlos. "Cemetery, Ninth Ward, and Magazine Street today, what do you think?" she asked.

"You're in charge, baby," Carlos said.

Carlos paid for the coffee and they piled into Judah's Mini Cooper.

//

On the bus ride back to St. Louis, Izzy reflected on the trip. It had started out a little rocky but once Judah had taken over, they had a blast. She felt like she had seen everything there was to see in New Orleans. She reached over and squeezed Carlos's hand.

"Great honeymoon, baby," she said. "The best."

Five

IZZY

WHEN THEY RETURNED FROM NEW ORLEANS, MR. PICKLES wasn't waiting at the door for Izzy. She looked under her bed and in all of the closets. From her bedroom window she could see Carlos in the parking lot, loading the last of her boxes into the back of his van.

Izzy walked around the house calling the cat. "Here, kitty-kitty. Mr. Pickles, where are you?"

Izzy stomped into the living room where Dotty was dozing in her favorite chair.

"Mom," Izzy said. "Mom, wake up."

Dotty snorted and opened one eye. "What is it?"

"What did you do with Mr. Pickles?" Izzy demanded.

"The cat?" Dotty wasn't quite awake. "Oh. He disappeared right after you left for New Orleans."

"What?" Izzy cried. "Did you forget to feed him?"

"I'm telling you he disappeared," Dotty said.

"Did you put food out for him?" Izzy asked.

"And attract rodents?" Dotty was awake now and angry. "No, I did not put food out for him."

Izzy screamed and ran out to the parking lot.

"What's wrong?" Carlos asked, startled.

"Mr. Pickles is missing," Izzy said.

"Oh, geez," Carlos said. "I almost forgot about him."

"My mom threw him out when we left for New Orleans," Izzy said. "She left him outside with no food for a week."

"He has got to be around here somewhere," Carlos. "Why don't you go next door and ask the neighbors if they have seen him?"

Izzy ran next door and rang the bell.

Mrs. Ramirez peered from behind the curtain and opened the door.

"Izzy, are you okay?" Mrs. Ramirez asked.

Izzy face was streaked with tears. "Have you seen my cat, Mr. Pickles? The big fat Siamese?"

"Yes," Mrs. Ramirez said. "I've seen him a couple of times hanging around the trash cans in the back alley. I didn't know he had run away."

"I was away on my honeymoon and he has been missing all week," Izzy said.

Mrs. Ramirez thought for a moment. "Why don't you ask Rona, she has all those cats and leaves food all over the place," she said. "Good luck, dear."

Izzy ran down the sidewalk to Rona's door. Rona! Why hadn't she thought of that? Rona was the crazy cat lady down the street. Of course! Mr. Pickles must have moved in with her.

Izzy was out of breath when she rang Rona's doorbell.

When Rona opened the door, Izzy was taken aback by the overwhelming odor.

"Hi, Rona," Izzy said. "My cat, Mr. Pickles, is missing and I wondered if maybe you had seen him?"

"What does he look like?" Rona asked. "Is he a big Siamese?"

"Yes, that's him!" Izzy said. "Have you seen him?"

"Yes, dear," Rona said. "He showed up at the back door about a week ago and I put food out for him. After a couple of days, he agreed to come inside. He's napping in the laundry room. Come in and get him. Do you have a carrier?"

Izzy was so relieved to have found Mr. Pickles that she did her best to ignore the squalor of Rona's house. She followed Rona down the hallway to the laundry room, carefully picking her way around overflowing litter boxes and dirty dishes, encrusted with rotting cat food. There was Mr. Pickles, napping on a pile of dirty laundry. She saw several other cats as well, perching on top of the washer, the dryer, and on the windowsills.

"Mr. Pickles!" Izzy kneeled down and pulled Mr. Pickles to her chest. He groaned in protest. "Are all these cats yours?" she asked.

"Do cats really belong to anybody?" Rona asked. "Just like Mr. Pickles, they show up and stay as long as they please. Now, how are you going to get him home?"

"I'll tell Carlos to come pick us up," Izzy said. She took out her phone and texted Carlos.

I found Mr. Pickles! Can you pick us up?

Carlos responded, Where are you?

"What's your house number?" Izzy asked Rona.

"Eleven twenty-eight," Rona said.

Down the street at #1128, Izzy texted.

Be right there, he replied.

Izzy struggled to carry Mr. Pickles to the front porch. Carlos was pulling up in his van.

"Thank you so much for taking him in," Izzy said to Rona and she climbed into the passenger seat. "Can we pay you for the week of food and litter?"

Carlos pulled a twenty from his wallet and

passed it out the window. Rona took the bill and slipped it inside her bra.

"You won't believe how many cats she has in there!" Izzy said as Carlos pulled away from the curb. "Did you get the last box out of my bedroom?"

"Yep, we're all packed and ready to move into my room," Carlos said. "Did you want to stop by to say good-bye to your mom?"

"Good riddance to bad rubbish!" Izzy said, indignant. "I read that somewhere in a book. My God, she abandoned Mr. Pickles! Who does that? And besides, she is probably passed out."

"This is why you are moving in with my family," Carlos said.

///

As Carlos pulled up in front of his house, he said, "You know, I never really talked to my mom about the cat. I guess I should go in and ask her if it's okay."

"If it's okay?" Izzy demanded. "I have a cat! You never told your mom?" Izzy was livid. How could Carlos have forgotten about Mr. Pickles? *He is all I will have in the world once Carlos is gone.*

"I never thought about it," Carlos said. "You could have mentioned it!" He was shouting now.

"What if she says no?" Izzy screamed. "What's our plan B?"

"There is no plan B!" Carlos yelled.

Just then, Carlos's brother, Oscar, walked up to the van. Carlos had asked him to help with the unloading. Oscar knocked on the driver's side window.

"What's going on, man?" Oscar asked.

Carlos rolled down the window. "Izzy has a cat," Carlos said. "I forgot to tell Mom about the cat."

"I'm sure she won't care," Oscar said. "Pop the back door and I'll start unloading. C'mon, I want to get this over with. My band has practice at three."

See, Izzy thought. *She won't care if I have a cat. Carlos, you are such a jerk sometimes!*

Carlos popped the latch and strode angrily toward the house.

"Mom?" he shouted.

"Is Izzy here?" Gilda asked.

"Yes," Carlos said. "And we forgot to mention, she has a cat. Can she bring the cat?"

"Of course," Gilda said. "This is her home now."

"Thanks, Mom," Carlos said, relieved. "I was so scared you were going to say no and Izzy would kill me."

Izzy appeared at the front door, struggling under the weight of Mr. Pickles.

"Who is this big fella?" Gilda asked.

"Mr. Pickles," Izzy said.

"Hello, Mr. Pickles," Gilda said. "Go ahead and put him in the bathroom while the boys are unloading. He must be distressed."

Six

IZZY

"THANK YOU, MRS. MORAN," Izzy said.

"Call me Mom," Gilda said. "You're in our family now."

Tears stung the back of Izzy's eyes. She blinked hard to keep the tears from flowing. She had never really felt as though her own mother liked her, much less loved her. Izzy had always thought that maybe she had been an unplanned pregnancy, an unwanted child. At the same time she felt overwhelmed at the prospect of being part of a big, loving family. It was too much; she felt unworthy of their attention and she didn't know how to respond. Carlos was the first person who had ever made her feel truly loved. She was resistant to his affections at first, afraid of sharing her feelings, afraid of being hurt. Only over a period of many months had she come to trust his love and learn how to love him in return.

//

The Morans lived in a low-slung brick ranch house with a fenced backyard that backed up to an open field. Across the field, there was a chain of high voltage power line towers. Izzy sat on the back patio and drank sweet tea while Carlos and Oscar unloaded the van and moved Izzy's stuff into Carlos's room. Mr. Moran had repainted Carlos's room and removed his desk and bookcase to make room for a queen-size bed and an extra dresser for Izzy's clothes. That night, Carlos and Izzy lay in bed with Mr. Pickles snuggled between them, purring.

"This is really happening, isn't it?" Izzy asked.

"What do you mean?" Carlos asked.

"Up until now, it all seemed so abstract to me," she said. "Get married, have a baby, join the Marines—it sounded like something that other people do. But this is us."

"Will you be okay living here without me?" Carlos asked as he nuzzled her neck.

"We never even got to live together, to play house," Izzy said. "This is all happening so fast."

"We'll do that," Carlos said. "When I get back—I promise. We'll get our own apartment and instead of a rubber doll we can play house with our very own baby."

"That's right," Izzy reassured him through her tears.

"Meanwhile, you've got Mr. Pickles," Carlos said.

"Your mom is the best for letting us move in," Izzy said.

"Are you kidding?" Carlos said. "She's thrilled to have you here. And I'll be back in October. Geez,

you'll be six months pregnant by then. Amazing!"
Carlos squeezed Izzy tight.

///

The next day, Carlos left for Parris Island, South
Carolina, for Marine Corps basic training. Izzy
drove him to the airport and stood beside the van
as Carlos unloaded his luggage from the back.

Izzy stood with the car keys in her hand and
watched Carlos walk through the automatic doors.
He turned once to wave at her and then he was
gone. Gone. She drove slowly home. She and
Carlos had been inseparable since tenth grade.
And now, he seemed excited to be leaving—well
of course, he was off to a new adventure. She, on
the other hand was stuck in St. Louis, without a
job or anything to look forward to.

///

"Izzy, is that you?" Gilda called out when the screen door slammed.

"Yeah," Izzy said. "I'm home." She flopped down onto the sofa next to Carlos's brothers Oscar and Willie. "What are you watching?" she asked.

"Cardinals versus White Sox," Oscar said.

"Did Carlos get off okay?" Gilda asked as she walked into the room.

"I guess so," Izzy said. "I dropped him at the curb. He would have called if the flight was cancelled or something. He's gone." She started to cry. Mr. Pickles jumped into her lap. "Ow, not on my bladder," Izzy said, shoving him aside.

"What's up with you?" Oscar said.

"Leave her alone," Gilda said. "She's missing Carlos. We'll all miss him."

"I won't," Oscar said.

"Izzy, come help me make lunch for the boys," Gilda said.

Izzy went into the kitchen where Gilda had laid

out bread and packages of cold cuts. Following Gilda's orders she made up plates of sandwiches.

"What are you going to do with yourself for the next six months?" Gilda asked. "You don't want to lie around the house, moping. You need to find a job."

"What kind of job?" Izzy moaned. "Who would hire a girl that is pregnant?"

"Doesn't your cousin, Nina, have a salon?" Gilda asked. "Maybe she needs help?"

Izzy munched on a potato chip and thought about it. "That's actually a really cool idea. I'll text her," Izzy said.

Mr. Pickles followed Izzy down the hall to her bedroom. She climbed onto her bed and opened her laptop.

Izzy texted Carlos, Miss you

No response.

"He's probably still on the plane," she said to Mr. Pickles.

Next, she texted Nina, Do you need any help at the shop?

Nina replied, Hey kid. How are you?

I need a job, Izzy texted.

Your timing is perfect! Nina texted. Bev just quit.

Can I come by today? Izzy asked.

Yes!

That night, Izzy sat alone in her room in front of her computer. She logged onto Facebook and searched for Marine wives. Then she searched for pregnant Marine wives. Then she searched for pregnant teens, and that's when she came across a group called Nine Months. She scrolled through the posts and checked out the profiles. Luciana was fourteen and wasn't sure who the father was. Jasmine was a nineteen-year-old college freshman from New Jersey. Aleecia was fifteen and Shawna and Candy were both eighteen. Shawna was getting married; the others were not.

Izzy rested her fingers on the keyboard for several minutes while she thought about whether to post something. Mr. Pickles rubbed up against her belly.

"It's just us now, Mr. Pickles," she said as she rubbed the soft spot behind his right ear.

Izzy started typing.

Izzy: Carlos left for Basic Training today.

Shawna: Is that your baby-daddy?

Izzy: Yeah. Well, he's my husband. We've been married for 2 weeks.

Aleecia: And now he's gone?

Izzy: For 12 weeks. And then off to Afghanistan, I guess. I'm so lonely.

Jasmine: How old are you?

Izzy: 18.

Candy: Me too.

Shawna: 2 weeks? Did you have a honeymoon?

Izzy: We went to New Orleans. It was fun, I guess.

Luciana: When is the baby due?

Izzy: February.

Aleecia: You aren't alone. We're here.

Izzy sent friend requests to all of the girls so they would show up in her feed. Then she checked out Carlos's Facebook. She scrolled through his photos of their wedding and the honeymoon. He had posted some new ones too. He had taken a photo of the G-shock Gravitymaster watch on his wrist. It looked like he had taken it from inside the plane. Below the photo he had posted a note: "I'll never take it off. Love you Izzy!" Seeing his smiling face in the photos just made her miss him more. She slammed her laptop shut.

"I need to get out of here," she said to Mr. Pickles.

Seven

IZZY

NINA SHOWED IZZY AROUND THE SALON AND WALKED her through her duties—sweeping the floor, booking appointments, doing laundry, and cleaning, cleaning, cleaning.

"Will you teach me how to shampoo?" Izzy asked.

"You need to register with a cosmetology school," Nina said. "Once you have your permit, I'll teach you how to wash and blow dry. Are you thinking of making a career of this?"

"Yeah, why not?" Izzy asked. "You make a pretty good living."

"It's hard work," Nina said. "Long hours on your feet. But, yeah, I like being my own boss and I have built up a solid base of customers. It would be nice if you would join the business. That would save me from hiring someone new every couple of months."

"What happened to Bev?" Izzy asked.

"She got poached by another salon and quit with no notice," Nina said. "They all quit. Constant turnover. I was freaking out just before I got your text. You are a life-saver!"

///

Nina was right, Izzy thought. It was hard work; she was exhausted by the time they locked up for the night. But she had been so busy, she hadn't had a chance to check her messages all day and there were a bunch from Carlos.

Just arrived.

Are you there?

Everything okay?

Call me when you get this!

She dialed Carlos's cell and got his voicemail.

"Sorry, baby," Izzy said into the phone. "I was working all day. Just heading home now. Call me. Love you."

She texted Carlos, I got a job!

After a few minutes, he responded, Can't talk right now—where are you working?

I'm working for my cousin, Nina, Izzy replied. It was your mom's idea.

He responded with a smiley face and a kiss emoji.

A few minutes later, he sent another text: What's the difference between the Air Force, the Army, the Navy and the Marines?

Izzy texted back: I don't get it. What?

Carlos replied, It's a joke.

Izzy texted, Okay what's the difference?

Carlos replied, When they are told to 'secure the building', the Army will post guards around the place, the Navy will turn out the lights and lock the doors. The Marines will kill everybody inside and set up a headquarters. The Air Force will take out a 5 year lease with an option to buy.

Izzy giggled and texted, LOL.

Here's another one, Carlos texted. How do you break up a bingo game in Afghanistan?

Izzy texted, How?

Carlos answered, Call out B-52.

Izzy texted, That's terrible! Where are you getting this stuff?

Carlos replied, Gotta go, sweetie. Be good.

///

One morning Izzy entered the kitchen and found Gilda doubled over in pain.

"What is it?" Izzy asked.

"I don't know," Gilda said. "It comes and goes."

"Where does it hurt?" Izzy asked.

"Everywhere," Gilda moaned. "Help me lie down."

Izzy helped Gilda hobble to the living room where she sank onto the couch and curled into a fetal position.

"I'll get Oscar," Izzy said. "Wait right here; I'll be right back."

Izzy dashed out to the backyard and found Oscar shooting hoops with Willie. "There's something wrong with Gilda!"

They ran back to the house and Oscar ran to his mom's side. "Mom, what is it? Can you talk?" To Izzy, he shouted, "Call 911! Get my dad!"

Izzy whipped out her phone and punched in 911 as she raced down to the basement to find Mr. Moran napping.

"What's your emergency?" the voice on the phone asked.

"Mr. Moran!" Izzy tugged on his sleeve. "There's something wrong with Mrs. Moran."

"What is your emergency?" the voice on the phone repeated.

Izzy spoke into the phone. "She's sick, she needs

an ambulance." Izzy repeated the address for the operator.

"Don't hang up until the EMT arrives," the voice said. "Stay with her and tell me what is happening."

Izzy followed Mr. Moran upstairs where Gilda was writhing on the couch. She howled when Ricardo tried to touch her.

"Is the ambulance coming?" Oscar asked.

"They're on their way," Izzy said. She had never seen Ricardo look so scared and that scared her.

Within minutes, they heard the sound of the approaching siren. Oscar rushed to the door and the emergency technicians were a blur of efficiency as they calmed Gilda, loaded her onto a stretcher and whisked her away. Mr. Moran rode in the back of the ambulance.

"What is it?" Izzy asked.

"The EMT said something about appendicitis," Oscar said. "But wait, that can't be right, she had her appendix out three years ago. We should go to the hospital."

//

At the hospital, Ricardo was sitting in the waiting room, his head in his hands.

"How is she?" Izzy asked.

"They don't know," Ricardo said. "They are running tests."

A few minutes later, a nurse walked into the room.

"You can see her now, Mr. Moran," she said.

Ricardo, his two sons, and Izzy followed the nurse through the door, and down the hall to Gilda's room.

"Not all at once," the nurse cautioned. "One or two at a time."

Ricardo went into the room while the others waited in the hall. After fifteen minutes or so, he re-emerged and ushered Oscar and Izzy in. Izzy stood at the foot of Gilda's bed. Oscar leaned over and kissed his mother.

"Mom, how are you?" Oscar whispered.

"Better," she said. "They gave me something for the pain and they're running a bunch of tests. Don't worry about me. I'm sure it's nothing."

Gilda managed a weak smile.

Oscar kissed his mother on the cheek. "Bye, Mom," he said.

///

Gilda was released the following morning and Oscar, Willie, and Izzy sat on the front steps, watching for his father's car. Izzy held Mr. Pickles in her lap.

"Here they come!" Izzy cried. She jumped to her feet. Mr. Pickles hissed and scrambled.

///

Ricardo helped Gilda out of the car and into their bedroom. When he came back out he summoned the boys and Izzy into the living room.

"Sit down," he said. The three sat together on the couch.

"She has cancer," Ricardo said. "Pancreatic." The words hung in the air like a leaky helium balloon slowly succumbing to gravity. *Pancreatic cancer!* Izzy thought. *I need to call Carlos.*

Ricardo read her mind. "I'll call Carlos's Commanding Officer and get the message to him."

Izzy's phone buzzed an hour later. It was Carlos.

"Hi baby," Izzy said. "Did you talk to your dad?"

"Yeah," Carlos said. "Tell me everything. What exactly happened? Has she been sick before?"

"No, yesterday was the first time I ever saw her sick," Izzy said. "She never said anything about feeling sick. We're just as shocked as you. Will they let you come home now?"

"I'll be done with Basic in two months," Carlos

said. "I'll put in for hardship leave to see if I can spend a little more time with you before we're deployed."

Izzy's heart sank.

"Call me every day and tell me what's happening. Surgery, chemo, the whole thing," he said.

"And with me and the baby, right?" Izzy asked. "Every day something is new with us."

"Of course, sweetie," Carlos said.

Eight

CARLOS

IT WAS STILL HOTTER THAN HADES IN SOUTH CAROLINA EVEN though it was September, and Carlos, who prided himself on his fitness—after all he had been a starter with the basketball and baseball teams—found himself nauseous after the ten-mile run his platoon did after breakfast every morning. He was conscious that he was building muscle while at the same time losing weight and, overall, he enjoyed the aggressive competition of Basic Training. He savored the feeling of falling into bed every night with every muscle and joint aching. In Basic, every minute was scheduled,

programmed. You knew exactly where you were supposed to be and what you were supposed to be doing.
And every performance was ranked and scored. Carlos
liked the immediate feedback. And he was also glad
that he had very little time to himself to worry about
his mother's chemo and Izzy's advancing pregnancy. He
had promised to Skype with Izzy every day. Still, three,
maybe four days would go by before he would notice
some other soldier firing up his laptop in the barracks.
In those moments he would be wracked with guilt.

As soon as he clicked on the Skype icon, he
would hear the accusatory tone, alerting him that
Izzy was online. She kept her phone on at all
times during the day—at the salon, in the kitchen
making dinner for the family, and at night in bed.

"Hey, baby!" Izzy cried.

To Carlos, her face looked puffy, possibly dis-
torted by the low-res web cam on her laptop.

"You've lost weight!" she cried.

Carlos laughed and flexed a bicep. "Solid muscle,
babe," he said. "How is Mom doing?" he asked.

Nine

IZZY

IZZY WAS HURT. THAT WAS ALWAYS HIS FIRST QUESTION. How was Gilda doing? Not how she was doing. Not how much he missed her.

"I'll get her in a minute," Izzy said. "She wants to talk to you, too."

How did married people talk to each other? she wondered. She thought about Ricardo and Gilda—they obviously loved each other but their conversations, at least the ones she had overheard, never ventured past logistics. What's for dinner? Can you take the car into shop for repairs? Did you pay the phone bill? But there was something unspoken as well—a softness in the way they looked at each other, the occasional gentle caress, the occasional embrace. In this Skype environment, she thought there needed to be more—something to keep the love alive—some flirting, some sexting, some exposure—she thought about unbuttoning her blouse and slipping her bra strap off of her shoulder. But then she was scared that somebody might be looking over Carlos's shoulder. She didn't want to embarrass him and in doing so, humiliate herself.

"Do you miss me?" Izzy asked.

"Of course I do," Carlos said. "You're all I think about."

Izzy wondered, *why don't you Skype me more often, then*? But she bit her tongue.

"How was your day?" she asked.

"Every day is the same," Carlos said. "Endurance run, calisthenics, obstacle course, rifle range. How was your day?"

"Wash towels, sweep up hair clippings," she paused. "We need to find something else to talk about."

"How is the baby?" Carlos asked.

Izzy stood up to focus the webcam on her baby bump.

"Wow!" Carlos said. "That's awesome!"

Izzy sat back down to face the screen. "What are we naming her?" she asked.

"Her?" Carlos asked. "Are you sure it's a girl?"

"Her, him," Izzy said. "What are we naming our baby?"

"What about Carla if it's a girl and George, if it's a boy?" Carlos suggested.

Izzy thought for a moment. *George,* she thought. *That's nice.*

"I like that," she said. "Good choices." Her voice softened. "Talk to me about the future."

"The future?" Carlos asked.

"I don't know," Izzy said. "Tell me a story— with a fairy-tale ending. Like . . . you come home from Afghanistan in one piece and you are a war hero and, and, and we buy a little house in the suburbs and we have two kids who play soccer and little league."

"And what else?" Carlos asked.

"Let's see, you'll go into business with your dad and I'll open my own day-spa," Izzy said. "And our kids will be smart and popular and athletic. And happy, we'll all be really, really happy."

The Skype connection started to freeze.

"Carlos?" Izzy cried. "Can you hear me? Call me back!"

Gilda poked her head in the door. "Is Carlos on the line? Can I talk to him?"

"He was here a second ago," Izzy said. "Let me try to reconnect." Izzy clicked on the call button again and waited. Carlos's face came into view.

"Mom!" he cried.

Izzy stood up and held the chair for Gilda. "I'll give you two some privacy," she said. She stepped into the hallway. But she couldn't help herself; she stood just outside to listen.

"What's the latest with the treatments?" Carlos was asking. "How are you feeling?"

"The doctor said the chemo isn't working," Gilda said. "He wants to try something new."

"I'll be done with Basic in a month," Carlos said. "I put in for hardship leave. I'll come home for a week before we're deployed."

"Where are they sending you?" Gilda asked. Her voice was shaking.

"Mom, you know I don't know that yet," Carlos said. "How is Izzy doing?"

"She is such a good girl," Gilda said. "She is a big help to me but I think she is very lonely. I worry for her. At her age, she should be out with friends instead of hanging out on Facebook chatting with those girls."

"What girls?" Carlos asked.

Izzy suppressed a gasp of surprise.

"She found some Facebook group for teen moms," Gilda said.

"What?" Carlos sounded shocked. "She's not a

teen mom—well I mean, sure she's eighteen and she's going to be a mom but teen moms . . . aren't those unwed mothers?"

"That's what I'm saying," Gilda said. "None of her friends are married or having babies. She's all alone here."

"What are they talking about on Facebook?" Carlos asked.

"Who knows. Abortion, adoption, you name it," Gilda said. "I don't think it's healthy."

"Oh my God!" Carlos said. "What the hell is she talking to a bunch of—" he stopped himself. "I'll talk to her about getting out more," he said, closing the book on the subject.

Izzy gasped audibly. Had Gilda been stalking her on Facebook? She tiptoed down the hall and locked herself in the bathroom. She sat on the toilet holding her head. Her face was hot, her mouth was dry, and she could hear the blood pounding inside her head. Gilda had betrayed her. Even her own mother had never stalked her on Facebook. And talking with Carlos about her behind her back? Her mind raced—she wanted to run away—but where would she go?

She heard a gentle knock on the door.

"Izzy?"

It was Gilda.

"Izzy, are you in there? Are you okay?"

Izzy took a deep breath. She stood up and turned on the faucet. She stared at her face in the mirror, which looked pasty, drained of all color, and puffy—like a doughy biscuit. She reached back and flushed the toilet.

"In a minute," Izzy called out.

When she opened the door, the hallway was empty. She walked back to her bedroom and quietly shut the door. She flicked off the overhead light and crawled under the covers, fully dressed. She curled up in a ball and buried her head between two pillows, clenching her eyes tight.

Ten

IZZY

THE NEXT FOUR WEEKS PASSED QUICKLY FOR IZZY. Carlos was coming home today!

Ric took the boys to the airport to meet Carlos's flight. Izzy stayed home with Gilda who was too weak to get out of bed.

Izzy sat by Gilda's bed with a cup of ice chips in case she stirred and seemed thirsty. She checked the messages on her phone every few minutes. She looked at Gilda to see whether she was sleeping. *Can I run down the hall real quick and grab my laptop?* Yes, she thought she could.

She dashed to her room, opened her laptop, and logged onto Facebook, hoping the other girls were there.

Jasmine had posted photos of her baby, taken shortly after birth.

Izzy: OMG! Is that Orchid?

Shawna: She's so beautiful!

Jasmine: Thanks! She smells so sweet, I could just gobble her up!

Luciana: Anybody heard from Candy lately? Do you think she's OK?

Candy: Sorry guys, I've been on bed rest—all I do is sleep and sometimes I lose track of the days. I'm still here—just being a human incubator.

Aleecia: Human incubator—I love that! That's exactly what it feels like.

Izzy: Carlos is coming home today!

Aleecia: He finished with basic training already? That was fast!

Izzy: Not to me! It feels like forever. I hope I'll recognize him.

Jasmine: Silly! I'm sure he'll recognize you.

Izzy: Does anybody else know that you are on this group? Kyle? Danilo? Eddie?

Aleecia: No! Why?

Candy: What happened?

Izzy: Apparently my mother-in-law was snooping around online and discovered my posts. She told Carlos and he freaked out. He thinks I'm going to get an abortion or adoption or something.

Shawna: When did he find out?

Izzy: Last month. And he hasn't mentioned it once, since. I'm kind of scared to see him today.

Jasmine: Why, what's wrong with talking to your friends on Facebook?

Izzy: Yeah, but you're my 'teen mom' friends.

Jasmine: Exactly, you need friends to share your experiences with. I don't know anybody who is going through this but you all.

Luciana: Me neither.

Candy: If it weren't for you guys, I would be all alone.

Aleecia: I guess I'm lucky. I have my prego group at school.

Izzy: OMG! I think I hear the car—gotta go!

Izzy slammed her laptop shut and dashed back toward Gilda's room, stopping to appraise her reflection in the mirror hanging on the back of her closet door.

What a mess! she thought. Frizzy hair, puffy face, swollen ankles, and a shapeless maternity sack-dress that she had picked up at the Goodwill store. Why pay good money for something you'll only wear for a few months? That was Gilda's advice. Now, Izzy found herself wishing she had splurged on one nice outfit. This was not how she wanted Carlos to see her for the first time in months. She made one last tug at her unfortunate hemline, squared her shoulders and marched down the hall with a brave smile on her face.

Carlos was sitting in the chair next to Gilda's bed and holding her hand. He was speaking softly to her. Her eyes were open and fixed on him.

"Hi," Izzy said, shyly.

Carlos turned to look at her. He wasn't smiling. "Where were you?" he asked.

"I've been here all day—sitting right in that chair," Izzy said, flustered. "I . . . just had to go to the bathroom. I was only gone a minute." Was he accusing her of abandoning Gilda? Why did Gilda's feelings always come first?

"There's a bathroom right here," Carlos said. "Why did you use the one down the hall?"

Izzy thought fast. "My hairbrush is in the other bathroom," she said. "I wanted to look pretty for you. Do I?"

Carlos looked her up and down. He gave a hint of a smile. "Of course, you do," he said at last. "You always look pretty."

"Can I have a hello kiss?" Izzy asked.

"Sure," Carlos said. He squeezed Gilda's hand and lay it gently back on her ribs. He stood up to face Izzy and took her face in his hands and kissed her. "You smell great."

"Thank you." To Gilda, she said, "Can I get you anything? Some ice chips? A little bite to eat?"

Gilda smiled and shook her head. She made a shooing motion with her hand and Izzy led Carlos out of the room and into the kitchen.

"I had no idea how bad it was," Carlos said. He started to cry. "I miss her so much." He pressed his fingertips to his eyes.

Izzy's heart rose in her chest and she couldn't breathe. She understood how painful this must be for Carlos. At the same time, though, she had been in this house, all alone, with his baby growing in her stomach. She nearly screamed, *What about me?*

"She's so small," Carlos continued. "She doesn't look like my mom, at all. I almost couldn't recognize her."

Izzy put her hand on Carlos's arm. Wow, his bicep was hard! *Wait, wait, I should say something,* she thought, but she couldn't think of anything so she just continued to caress his arm.

Carlos let out a big sigh and looked at her. "I'm

sorry if I sounded mad before," Carlos said. "My dad told me how good you've been to her. He said you have been a huge help." He put his arm around her and pulled her close. "Man, you've gotten fat!" He laughed, his eyes still wet with tears.

"Thanks a lot!" Izzy said. "Just because you've gotten buff."

Carlos laughed again and hugged her with both arms. Izzy was amazed at the change in his physique—his abs were so hard, his chest was twice as big as his waist. *He's like a Ken doll!* she thought.

//

That night as they lay in bed, Carlos caressed Izzy gently, as though she was made of porcelain and might shatter.

"Is this okay?" Carlos asked. He pressed his erection against her thigh. "Will we hurt the baby?"

"The doctor says it's fine," Izzy said. She savored his scent and the strength of his embrace. "Just don't put all your weight on me." He rolled her over and entered her from behind. She wanted him to go on forever.

"I've missed you so much," she said. Just then he finished.

Carlos flopped over onto his back and Izzy rolled toward him, cradling her head against his collarbone.

"I miss you, too, baby," Carlos said. "You are the best."

"When do you have to leave?" Izzy asked. "Did you get a hardship pass?"

"I need to be back on base next week for some more training," Carlos said. "They said I could take hardship leave when my mom is on her deathbed."

"What about when your wife is giving birth?" Izzy asked.

"You know, I asked about that," Carlos said. "Not so much."

"Seriously?" Izzy was appalled. *You can come home if your mom is dying but not if your wife is giving birth?* That means if she got lucky, Gilda would die the same week her baby was born. Right after that thought entered her mind she started to hate herself for even thinking it.

//

At her next doctor's appointment, Dr. Millman rolled the ultrasound wand across Izzy's abdomen and asked, "Would you like to know the sex?"

"You can tell already?" Izzy asked. She wondered what Carlos would say. Would he want to know? He should be here for this. Her heart was leaden. "Sure."

Eleven

CARLOS

CARLOS DIDN'T LIKE THE LOOKS OF THINGS AS HIS three-helicopter convoy of Chinooks scudded low over the Afghanistan countryside flying into an increasingly ugly sandstorm. The pilot was having difficulty handling the chopper because of the heavy sling load they carried beneath them: two containers of critical spare parts for helicopters that had been damaged in a firefight the night before. Trying to avoid the weather, they had drifted a few miles east of their intended course into enemy territory and were still about forty miles from their destination. Carlos closed his eyes and said a prayer for his mom, and then for Izzy. *I'm coming home to you, baby,* he thought. *I promise.*

The day before, the crowds in the villages below had waved and cheered as they flew from Camp Dwyer carrying troops and supplies to the new aviation base camp south of Kabul. But on this day, the crowds seemed more aggressive. From the cockpit jump seat of the second Chinook, Carlos saw people twirling white towels overhead in imitation of helicopter blades. White pickup trucks raced ahead of them, whirled around, and stopped while their passengers got out and stared. Then two men directly beneath ran over to a white Nissan pickup. One pulled out an AK-47 rifle, the other a hand-held rocket launcher and pointed it at the chopper.

"Shoot those fuckers!'" Carlos yelled to the gunner.

Clay, the co-pilot turned the controls over to Dan, the pilot-in-command.

Carlos felt a shudder, and a big boom. A missile

ripped into the back of the aircraft, tearing a softball-sized hole. Two AK-47 rounds hit them, too. One penetrated an electrical panel behind Carlos's seat, setting off whistles and alarms. The second pierced the left side of the aft ramp and ricocheted off a strut in the cabin. A chunk of that bullet hit Carlos in the cheek and Lance, the flight engineer, rushed to help him.

"I'm hit!" Carlos screamed. He was still conscious and sitting up, but his face was bleeding pretty badly.

"You okay, buddy?" Lance sounded like he was yelling from far away. Carlos nodded. Lance reached for a bundle of shop towels and pressed it against Carlos's cheek.

With Carlos injured, Dan made the call to return to base camp. *The Wizard of Oz* flashed into Carlos's mind as Dan tried to dump the load directly on top of the gunmen. He imagined crushing them like Dorothy's house crushed the wicked witch. He didn't know if Dan had succeeded.

With all three helicopters hearing gunfire and one already hit, the convoy headed west toward open country—and into an ever-worsening storm. Carlos's crew was no longer sure if they were under fire. The two other helicopters were flying alongside, trying not to run into each other. Finally, the first Chinook pilot decided he couldn't safely continue. Carlos heard the call over the radio. "We have to land!" The lead helicopter slowed and dropped its containers from a height of ten feet before landing nearby. Hitting a wall of sand, Carlos's Chinook felt its way toward the ground, low and slow. Damage to the aircraft had affected its ability to brake and it landed hot and fast; the landing roll, normally one hundred feet or less, stretched to a quarter mile. Once they had landed, the crew secured the load, strapped Carlos into a gurney, set up guards, and called for help.

They sat there, fearful and tense, for over an hour until a UH-60 Black Hawk found them and escorted them to base where a doctor appeared at the door of the helicopter to attend to Carlos. Luckily, the bullet fragment had only nicked his cheek.

///

That evening after dinner, Izzy turned on the television to watch the news and get the latest update on military action in Afghanistan. The TV journalist was reporting in via satellite from Kabul.

"The first missile had hit the sling load, exploding that stuff," the reporter was saying. "It probably saved their lives. I was a passenger in the first Chinook. It opened up like a can opener."

The reporter then interviewed the Chinook's door-gunner, O'Keefe. "Thank God it didn't detonate. We expected maybe small-arms fire, but never rockets. This was a little more organized than pot shots," O'Keefe added.

The anchor said, "Sounds like good crew coordination helped save their lives."

"Everybody did exactly what they were supposed to do," O'Keefe said.

//

"It was almost like a shaving cut," Carlos said as he finished telling the story to Izzy via Skype.

"Wait a second! I think you were on the news tonight!" Izzy cried.

"What?" Carlos asked.

"Was there a reporter with you in the helicopter?" Izzy asked. "He said he was a passenger in the first Chinook."

"I was riding in the second bird," Carlos said. "But there was no reporter embedded in our convoy."

"He said you saved his life," Izzy said.

"That asshole?" Carlos said. "He was in another aircraft that came in behind us about thirty to forty-five minutes later. He shows up and starts spouting off that it was just like *Saving Private*

Ryan and that the whole army would be out looking for him. I called him an idiot in front of his camera crew. He left in a different flight of Chinooks from another unit and flew to Kabul."

"Yeah," Izzy said. "He said he was reporting from Kabul."

"Did Mom see it?" Carlos asked.

"No, she was asleep," Izzy said.

"Thank God," Carlos said. "Don't tell anybody that I was there, please?"

"But, aren't you a hero?" Izzy asked. "Won't they find out eventually?"

"They can find out after I'm back home, okay?"

"Okay, sweetie," Izzy said. "That must have been so crazy to be in the middle of that."

"It was. Like I was saying earlier," Carlos said. "We are used to the villagers waving at us when we fly in supplies for bridges and shit. That was some ugly shit yesterday."

Izzy could hear the fear in his voice and it scared her.

"But you're fine right?" Izzy said. "You'll be alright?"

"Man, I hope so," Carlos said. "I have to go, Izzy. You be good, okay?"

"Wait!" Izzy cried. "I forgot to tell you. It's a boy!"

"What?" Carlos exclaimed. "When did you find out?"

"I went for an ultrasound last week," Izzy said. "Everything is fine; he's healthy and growing like a weed. Here, look." Izzy held the printout of the ultrasound up to the computer screen.

"That's amazing!" Carlos said. "Hi, George, hi, baby George!"

There was a commotion behind Carlos. He craned his neck to see what it was.

"Baby, I gotta go," he said.

The screen went blank.

"Don't go!" Izzy pressed the palm of her hand to the computer screen. "Baby, please don't go," she whispered.

Twelve

IZZY

IZZY SAT IN THE WAITING ROOM OF GILDA'S DOCTOR'S office. This had never happened before. Usually, she wheeled Gilda into the chemo room and sat with her during the treatment. Today they had asked her to wait outside. Christmas tunes were playing on the intercom and she was transported back to last Christmas, the time when Carlos had proposed. She twisted the ring on her finger and thought, *so much has happened in a year*. Just then a nurse poked her head out of the door.

"Ms. Moran?" the nurse asked. "The doctor would like a word with you."

Izzy pushed herself awkwardly up out of the chair and waddled after the nurse. She was surprised to see Gilda sitting in the doctor's office in her wheelchair.

"Have a seat, Ms. Moran," Dr. Wolfman said. Izzy sat.

"The chemo isn't working," Gilda said.

Izzy gasped.

"Ms. Moran," Dr. Wolfman said. "As Gilda said, the combination of drugs that we have been using to arrest the growth of the tumor doesn't seem to be working any longer. We have seen significant growth since our last scan. Gilda has opted out of further treatment. She would like to be kept comfortable."

"Mom!" Izzy cried. Tears streaked her cheeks.

"I think it's important that we respect Gilda's choice and support her in every way possible." Dr. Wolfman said.

"Of course," Izzy said. She wiped her eyes and sat up straight. "What do I need to do?" she asked to nobody in particular. "It's just . . . " she said. "It's just that Carlos is deployed in Afghanistan. I don't know how to deal with all of this. I'm sorry, Gilda, but I don't. He should be here with you."

"He's coming home," Gilda said.

"What?" Izzy cried. "When?"

"Sometimes when I can't sleep at night, I Skype with Carlos," Gilda said. "He said he had told you that they gave him leave—he'll be home for Christmas."

Well, he hadn't told me! Izzy thought, suddenly angry. *It's always about his mom. Why doesn't he tell me this stuff?* She had to stop herself from thinking these selfish thoughts.

"That's wonderful!" Izzy tried to sound enthusiastic.

//

Izzy sat in the cellphone lot at Lambert airport waiting for a text from Carlos. She opened the Facebook app on her phone and checked her feed.

Candy had posted photos of her son, Matteo.

Izzy: I'm having a boy, too! We're naming him George.

Candy: I like that name—George!

Izzy: Carlos is coming home today!

Shawna: For good?

Izzy: He got a five-day leave to visit his mom. She's really sick and we don't know how much time she has left.

Luciana: :(

Aleecia: Anybody hear from Jasmine lately?

Luciana: Didn't you hear? She gave Orchid up for adoption!

Izzy gasped. *Adoption?* Just then George kicked and she pressed her palm against her belly to feel if he would kick again. She couldn't imagine ever giving her son up for adoption. She wondered if she could find a way to contact Jasmine outside of the Facebook group. She was thinking of what to type when her phone buzzed. *Carlos is here!* She checked her hair and makeup in the rearview mirror before starting the van.

She spotted him immediately. He looked so tall and handsome in his fatigues, standing next to his duffel bag and peering intently at his phone. He didn't even look up as she approached. She put the van in park and ran around to him.

"Hey sailor!" she cried. "Need a lift?"

"Izzy!" Carlos smiled broadly and embraced her. "Oh my God, you're so big!"

"Eight months," Izzy said. "And he's kicking. Want to feel him?" She took his hand and placed it on her belly.

"I feel him!" Carlos said. "That's amazing!"

Carlos loaded his gear into the back of the van and took the wheel.

"How's Mom doing?" Carlos asked as soon as he pulled away from the curb.

"She's pretty much out of it all the time, now,"

Izzy said. "They have her on so much morphine, she doesn't really wake up any more."

"Will she even know that I'm here?" Carlos asked. His voice was shaking.

"We can ask the hospice nurse to turn down the morphine drip," Izzy said, flatly. "Your dad has been doing that. She'll wake up so he can talk to her for a bit until the pain becomes too much for her."

Carlos looked at her. "Are you okay?" he asked. "You sound upset."

"Upset?" Izzy asked. "I don't know, I guess I'm a little hurt that the military will grant you leave if your mom is sick but not if your wife is in labor. If Gilda could have hung on a couple more months, you'd be here for George's birth. Now who is going to be here for me? Not you, not Gilda, certainly not my mom." Izzy started to cry.

"Izzy," Carlos said, sympathetically. "You're in mourning. I know it's a shock."

"Am I?" Izzy cried. "Mourning for Gilda? Or

am I mourning for the father of my child who is seven thousand miles away. What about me, Carlos?" What about me?"

They rode in silence the rest of the way.

//

The house was hushed when they arrived. Ricardo met them at the door and silently embraced his son. They walked together into Gilda's room and shut the door, leaving Izzy standing in the hallway. She went to her room and climbed into bed.

//

"Izzy." Carlos was shaking her shoulder. "Don't you want to come down for dinner? Dad is cooking."

"What's he making?" Izzy asked. She was still groggy but her stomach was wide-awake.

"His specialty—pulled pork and rice," Carlos

said. He lay down on the bed and spooned her. "I'm sorry, Izzy. I know this isn't fair to you. I want to be here when George is born, you know I do. You are the most important person in the world to me; you know that."

"Sometimes it doesn't feel that way," Izzy said. "I didn't even know you were coming home this month—your mom told me."

"I did tell you," Carlos said. "On Skype? Are you having pregnancy brain?"

"You told me a bunch of stupid military jokes," Izzy said. "I remember that. Nothing about a leave."

"I'm sorry baby," Carlos said. "Don't be mad. Now, let's eat. Something smells great!"

///

In the morning, Gilda was gone. She had passed away peacefully in her sleep. The funeral was held two days later. And the following day Carlos was on a plane back to join his unit in Afghanistan.

Thirteen

IZZY

IZZY WAS ATTENDING COSMETOLOGY SCHOOL IN THE morning and working in the salon from two until five o'clock every day. Nina had started letting her cut hair—mostly just kids and the occasional male client. Nina and Izzy were both busy with clients when the front door opened and in walked Pete. Izzy hadn't seen him since high school. Pete had played on Carlos's baseball team. *Damn*, Izzy thought, *he looks great.*

"Hi, can we help you?" Nina called out, her scissors suspended in midair.

"Got time for a quick trim?" Pete asked.

"Pete?" Izzy asked. "It's Izzy."

"Izzy!" Pete said. "I didn't recognize you."

Izzy laughed. "I guess not!" she said. "Why don't you take a seat at the first sink and I'll get you washed."

Pete settled into the chair and rested his head on the rim of the sink. "I heard you and Carlos got married," Pete said. "But I didn't know you were having a baby."

Izzy tested the water temperature and ran the hose over Pete's head. "Due next month," Izzy said. "It's a boy. George."

"George Moran," Pete said. "That's a serious name. He could be a politician. Senator George Moran."

As Izzy gently massaged the shampoo into Pete's hair, she smiled at the thought of her son becoming somebody important, somebody famous. She caught her reflection in the mirror and did a double take. *When was the last time I smiled,* she wondered? *It seems like I have been sad forever.*

"What's Carlos up to?" Pete asked.

"He's in Afghanistan. He's a Marine," Izzy said.

"Oh, man," Pete said. "He left you here all alone? I mean—wow, that's pretty serious."

Izzy just smiled. "Let's get you into the chair."

Pete settled into the salon chair and Izzy covered him with a gown.

"What are we doing today?" Izzy asked.

"So you're a pro?" Pete asked. "You cut hair?"

"Well, you're my first," Izzy said. "Let's see how it goes."

Pete jerked upright.

"Silly!" Izzy said in a fit of giggles. "I'm teasing. Yes, I'm getting my certification. What are you up to?"

"I'm at UMSL," Pete said. "Majoring in Poli-Sci."

Izzy was running her fingers through Pete's hair and snipping.

"Funny running into you here," Pete said. "I've walked by this shop plenty of times. My apartment is just around the corner. How long have you been working here?"

"Since last summer," Izzy said. "Why did you stop in today? Big date tonight?"

"Actually, yeah," Pete said.

Izzy blushed. *Why am I blushing?* She was so embarrassed.

"I'm leading a protest march tomorrow," Pete said.

"Protest march? What are you protesting?" Izzy asked.

"Ironically, this fucking endless war in Afghanistan," Pete said. "Do you know how much it is costing us? And all the pointless loss of life? I hate to say it, and don't get mad, but why the fuck is Carlos over there? Does he believe in this shit?"

Izzy didn't know what to say. As a matter of fact, she didn't know what Carlos believed. She knew that he believed that joining the Marines would pay well and would lead to career opportunities and allow them to buy a house and have a comfortable life. She had no idea what his politics were or whether he had gone to war to fight for a cause. They had never discussed it. "I think it's just a job," she said.

"Really?" Pete barked. "Just a job? It's his job to slaughter innocent civilians and then maybe trip on an IED and lose his legs and never walk again, all in a day's work? Seriously?"

"I, uh, I don't like it," Izzy said. "I wish he wasn't over there. He was in a helicopter that was shot down. He got shot in the cheek. He said it wasn't anything but I worry about him every day. I worry that I'm making my baby sick because I'm stressed out and worried all the time." Izzy started to cry. "I hate the stupid war, too," she said.

"I'm sorry, Izzy," Pete said. "I didn't mean to make you cry. I shouldn't have said all that stuff. But if you feel so strongly about it, maybe you want to come to the protest tomorrow?"

Izzy wiped her eyes with a tissue. "Where is it?" she asked.

"Forest Park, South Entrance, ten a.m." Pete said. "Do you want me to pick you up?

Izzy thought about how awkward it would be if Ricardo saw Pete drive up to pick up his pregnant daughter-in-law. "No," she said. "I'll meet you there. South Entrance?"

"Follow the signs," Pete said. "Text me when you get there. What's your number?

Izzy read off her cell and Pete typed it into a text.

Her phone buzzed. Pete's text read, Nice job on the haircut

Izzy blushed.

Nina was standing at the front desk, waiting to cash Pete out.

After he had paid, he turned toward Izzy and said, "See you tomorrow, kid."

Nina waited until he was out the door and then asked, "What was that about?"

"He's leading a march in the park, tomorrow," Izzy said.

"What kind of march?" Nina asked.

"Something about the war," Izzy said.

"Izzy, your husband is a fucking Marine!" Nina said. "You can't go to a protest. You need to support him."

"I am supporting him," Izzy said. "I'm marching in support of him. Don't you think there will be other military wives there?"

"What are you talking about?" Nina said. "If you're against the war, you're against what he's doing. It's his job!"

"Is that what it is?" Izzy asked, echoing Pete. "It's just a job?"

///

The next morning, Izzy got up early and showered before Ric and the boys had stirred. She drove to Forest Park and found a parking spot on Washington Drive. As she turned off the van, she started to have second thoughts. *What would Carlos think if he knew I was here? Oh, fuck it.* She heard people chanting in the distance and she locked the van and headed in their direction.

Izzy was immediately swallowed in the crowd of protesters, chanting: "Hey hey, ho ho! This racist war has got to go! No more lining pockets of the corporations, fighting wars with smaller nations!"

She wasn't sure what the words meant. *If we're fighting wars with smaller nations, how come we always lose?* she wondered. But, she liked the rhythm and rhyme. She felt she was participating in something important, something meaningful. She wondered if that is how Carlos felt, waking up every day in a war zone. The group was heading off through the park and she started following when she felt a hand on her shoulder.

"Izzy!"

She turned to look. It was Pete.

"You came," he said. "I wasn't sure you would."

"Yes," Izzy said. "I'm here."

Pete took her hand and they joined a line of

about a hundred activists carrying coffins and signs reading "HANDS OFF SYRIA" and "WANTED FOR THE DESTRUCTION OF IRAQ."

A crowd had gathered around an elevated stage. Izzy could just barely make out the voice of the speaker.

"The invasion of Afghanistan is illegal under international law and constitutes an unjustified aggression," the speaker was saying. "Our continued military presence constitutes a foreign military occupation. The Taliban did not attack us on 9/11. Nineteen men, fifteen of them from Saudi Arabia, did, and there was no imminent threat that Afghanistan would attack the US or another UN member country. The war does nothing to prevent terrorism but increases its likelihood. This war is about geo-political and corporate interests."

Izzy had no idea what the speaker was talking about. "What corporate interests?" she asked.

Pete looked at her incredulously. "Where have

you been? Living under a rock? Oh right, busy making babies for your soldier."

Izzy was stung. *Why did Pete invite her here if he thought so little of her?* She looked back at the speaker. *What am I doing here?* She wondered.

Izzy's back started to ache. "I think I need to sit down," she said. She looked around. There was no place to sit, except on the frozen lawn. "I think maybe I should go."

"Do you want me to walk you to your car?" Pete asked.

"That's okay," Izzy said. "But thank you for inviting me. It was very interesting."

She thought she heard Pete snort and say under his breath, "Interesting, right!"

Fourteen

CARLOS

CARLOS'S REGIMENT, CARMIN 1, WAS PATROLLING THE Uzbin Valley to assess guerrilla activity. They were traveling with French troops along with elements of the Afghan National Guard. Their mission was to explore the area and make contact with local populations, in an effort to reinforce control of the region. The patrol was aware that there were enemy combatants in the valley but Carlos felt confident, knowing that the Americans were in charge of coordinating air support.

Carmin 1 bivouacked in a grove of cedar trees.

"This is bullshit," Lance said.

"What's bullshit?" Carlos asked.

"The fucking Italians," Lance said. "This sector had previously been under Italian control and was held up as a successful example of establishing security. It was supposed to be a quiet region despite the known presence of militants. Turns out the fucking Italian secret services were bribing local Taliban groups into inaction."

"Italian bribery?" Carlos said, sarcastically. "Shocking!"

"So here we are tagging along with the fucking French forces who were brought in to clean up the mess left by the Italians. Trying to cut off guerrilla groups from their rear bases in Pakistan. And risking our asses!"

"Fucking politics," Carlos said. "I just want to make it back home. I got a baby coming. I don't give a shit about the Italians or the French."

"Tell me about it, man," Lance said. "Let's get some shuteye. We head out at zero four hundred hours."

Before dawn, Carmin 1 headed for the mountain pass situated East of Uzbin Valley, leading to the heights of Sper Kunday. Two hours before the patrol reached the pass, the local Taliban leader was alerted and phoned local militants for support, making plans for an attack.

At an altitude of five thousand feet on the mountain pass, the American and French troops reached the end of the roadway.

"Evacuate your vehicles," the call commanded. "Advance on foot!"

Carmin 1 headed toward the pass along a narrow path while a French platoon bypassed Sper Kunday on the north.

Carlos's radio crackled to life.

"The French platoon has engaged a guerrilla group trying to surround the village," Carlos shouted to Lance.

Within minutes Carmin 1 came under fire from two guerrilla groups, north and south of their position.

"Hit the dirt!" Lance called out.

Carlos rolled behind a boulder and buried his head in the sandy soil, praying. *Please God, if I don't make it home, take care of Izzy and George for me.*

Carlos heard screams. He looked up and saw that Lance had been shot. He crawled over to Lance and rolled him over. He was dead, as were the radio operator and the Afghan interpreter.

In the distance, Carlos saw the French platoon storming to their rescue. But they came under fire from a third guerrilla group perched on a ridge above. With the death of the interpreter and wounding of four other Afghans, Carlos watched with dismay as the Afghan National Guard forces fled the scene, leaving the American and French troops alone.

Now disorganized, Carlos's regiment scrambled to find cover in the mountain brush, as more militants rushed towards their position in a pincer movement from the southern ridge. Well-trained snipers amongst the militants picked off the coalition forces while rocket-propelled grenades damaged three Afghan National Guard vehicles.

Carmin 1 dispersed over more than two hundred yards to find shelter and found themselves pinned down. From the valley below, the remaining French troops supported them by suppressing fire from their machine guns but Taliban units stormed a ridge north of the village on the rear of Carmin 1 and cornered the French armored unit.

"We need reinforcements!" Carlos shouted into his radio. Two F-15 fighters arrived a few minutes later. Hearing the fighter jets approaching, the Taliban closed in on the French positions, preventing the F-15s from firing, to avoid friendly fire casualties.

Meanwhile, Carmin 1 was dueling with the Taliban with hand grenades and sniper fire.

"We're running out of ammunition!" Carlos shouted to his CO. Just then his CO was struck by a bullet in the leg and killed by a second as he attempted to come to his rescue.

Fifteen

RICARDO

RICARDO KNEW IT HAD TO BE TERRIBLE NEWS WHEN THREE soldiers knocked on his door the next after-noon.

"It's Carlos!" he cried. "Izzy, Oscar, Willie, come quick!" He invited the soldiers into the living room. "Sit, please," he said.

Izzy arrived first. She was still in her robe and slippers. As soon as she saw the soldiers, she started to weep.

The casualty notification officers somberly relayed their message: Private Carlos Moran had perished in an ambush by the Taliban in the Uzbin Valley.

"Can you tell us what happened?" Ricardo asked. "How did he die?"

"I'm sorry, sir," Sgt. Sullivan said. "We don't have any more information at this time."

Izzy reeled with the shock. She couldn't comprehend what the soldiers were saying. "Is Carlos okay?"

Ricardo put his arm around her and pulled her close to him. "No, Izzy. No."

"I wish I had better news, that I didn't have to tell you this . . . " Sgt. Sullivan said. "These notifications . . . there is no easy way. An assistance officer will guide you through burial options, benefits, and other paperwork."

"What are you saying?" Izzy cried. "Carlos is dead?"

"Yes, ma'am, I'm sorry. You will be contacted within forty-eight hours. And there's also the Tragedy Assistance Program for survivors, a group that helps families who have lost a service member."

The soldiers quietly left the family to grieve.

"I'm just grateful that Gilda isn't here," Ricardo said. "If the cancer hadn't killed her, this surely would have."

//

It took weeks of calls and letters for Ricardo to finally get the full story on what had happened that awful day in the Uzbin valley.

Approximately thirty minutes after the air support had arrived, the French troops ran out of ammunition, and attempts at a counter-attack had to be aborted.

Air operations lasted for one hour, during which the remnants of Carmin 1 were able to reach the village. Two US Black Hawk helicopters then attempted to land to evacuate wounded, but were prevented by Taliban fire. Several hours later, helicopters previously reserved for a possible evacuation of Afghan President Hamid Karzai, arrived from Kabul and landed a physician and commandos. The helicopters quickly turned back and returned with four tons of ammunition, which was immediately carried to units under fire.

As the sun set, Carmin 1 was pinned down by Taliban fighters trying to surround the village. Their machine guns began to run low on ammunition again. As night fell, Predator drones guided mortar fire and another American regiment started climbing the pass to rescue the wounded and gather the dead while reinforcements from Kabul cleared the surroundings of the village. US aircraft pounded the surrounding ridges.

Around midnight, the sector was under control, firing around Sper Kunday had stopped, and the French and American troops had retaken the positions leading to the pass.

The first bodies were found at zero one-forty hours. Most of the bodies had been looted and some were discovered mutilated by the enemy. The last bodies were found in the morning. In all, nine soldiers had died and another eighteen were wounded.

The Taliban retreated into Laghman Province with their dead and wounded where they dispersed into three villages near the place of the ambush. NATO bombed these villages for three days, killing forty civilians, destroying one hundred and fifty houses and forcing two thousand people to flee.

It was later reported that an Afghan translator who accompanied Carmin 1 may have disappeared from the group "a few hours" prior to the ambush, stoking reports he may have been the one who alerted the militant commanders.

The Department of Defense said an investigation into the circumstances of the soldiers' deaths was under way.

Sixteen

IZZY

BAGPIPES WAILED IN THE BACKGROUND AS DOZENS OF soldiers and veterans with the Patriot Guard Riders stood in the rain outside Church of the Annunziata on a Monday morning, clutching towering poles topped with drenched American flags. The veterans carried bundles of American flags, handing them to passersby and drivers who pulled up alongside their small contingent in front of the church asking for them to mark their homes in memory of a fallen soldier who was a local boy. The veterans had decided to paint the town red, white, and blue for Moran.

"Who are the Patriot Guard Riders?" Izzy whispered to Nina.

"They are like Hells Angels except their mission is to attend funerals of soldiers and protect the family from protestors," Nina whispered back.

Izzy shot a guilty look at Pete, standing behind her. He squeezed her hand.

Lauren, a friend of Carlos's from church walked up to Izzy and hugged her. "Our house is decorated with yellow ribbons, and this is going right in front of the house," she said, clutching one of the flags. "We knew Carlos from our church group. As a friend, he was funny, athletic, and personable," Lauren said. "With gestures like the flag handout everyone can come together and remember him. I'm so sorry for your loss."

"Thank you for coming," Izzy said.

//

A young mother herded her two daughters along the sidewalk, each waving her own pennant. The older daughter bounced and waved the flag. "I'm going to put this on our mailbox!"

Her little sister said, "I want to plant mine in the ground in front of our house!"

Carlos's casket was carried into the church by a six-member honor guard.

The Very Reverend John Leykam spoke first. "We are gathered here today to honor the memory of Carlos Moran, a brave soldier who joined the Marines and was deployed to Afghanistan shortly after his eighteenth birthday. Carlos was a proud soldier and the kind of kid anyone would be proud to have as a son. You hear stories of casualties, and you feel bad, but when it happens to one of your own, it is devastating. We mourn his loss," he said.

Willie, Carlos's youngest brother, walked to the podium. "My brother Carlos was my inspiration, my hero, my role model, my life. You were the brightest star in the sky. Once a hero, always a hero."

Ricardo walked to the podium and led a round of applause in honor of the bravery of all the soldiers who have paid the ultimate sacrifice.

"As a former soldier, myself," Ricardo said, "I understand why Carlos joined the Marines. Even now, I respect and admire his decision. Carlos had an instinctual desire to serve his country. He had a passion and desire to explore the military . . . he pursued his dreams. He made himself and his family very proud with his selfless bravery. You have done your duty, son, and done it right to the last. If anyone here knew Carlos, you knew a respectable, kind, caring, thoughtful, smart, witty, and fun kid." Eulogizing his son, Ricardo said, "Carlos was as an old soul . . . old school. He loved the Rams, the Cardinals, flip cellphones, cigar magazines, the stock market, and conspiracy theories. 'I want to help people,' Carlos told me. You will always be loved and missed," Ricardo said as he began to choke up. "Thank you for giving your life for us all."

Oscar walked to the podium and held up Carlos's

dog tags. He read the inscription, "Greater love has no other than this, than to lay down your life for your friends." He flipped the tag over and read, "In memory of an American hero." Several people wiped away tears as Oscar spoke. "You will always be our hero, Carlos, thank you for the eighteen years you shared with us."

Major Genera Townsend took the podium. "The young soldier had a favorite quote: 'It's the journey, not the destination, that matters,'" Major Townsend said. "Anytime something happened to the platoon, Moran would scream about a conspiracy theory. One soldier joked that only Moran can actually make it sound real."

Everyone laughed.

"I want to share some stories I've heard from soldiers who knew Moran, including the time he entered a soldier's room spraying silly string. The soldier was angry until he realized it was Moran. Then there was the time Moran just got a new pair of sunglasses. He told everyone the glasses could see through the water and to the fish below," Townsend said. "Moran tried to demonstrate that and the glasses fell from his face into the water. His team got a good laugh. Another soldier, who had experienced a death in his family, struggled with the omnipresent death that came from being on the streets in Afghanistan. Moran helped him work through it. 'I am now and forever a better man because of Moran,' I recall him saying. He was commonly known among his fellow service members as 'Doc' or 'Doc Moran.'"

Townsend concluded with, "Some people say sports stars are heroes, some say movie stars are heroes. My heroes are the young Americans who wear the uniform of American military and law enforcement."

Hundreds of people stood in the streets outside and listened to the service. After, crowds broke into applause as the coffin was carried out. Army cadets lined the road outside the church and Veteran Standard Bearers formed a guard of honor with their flags as the coffin was carried into the churchyard.

Along the road, American flags fluttered from every lawn. Yellow ribbons and smaller flags marked each telephone pole.

When the Morans arrived back home, a wreath made with flowers and ribbons was propped next to the mailbox, and an American flag waved at half-staff next door. Down the block, a group of veterans stood on a street corner, chatting with flag recipients.

//

"In the space of a month, I've attended two funerals," Izzy said.

"Do you need to take some time off?" Nina asked. She watched Izzy attacking the hair clippings on the floor of the salon with a broom.

"No," Izzy said. "What am I going to do? Lie around in Carlos's old room and stare at the ceiling? I need to get out of there."

"Get out of there?" Nina asked. "You mean you want to move out?"

Izzy stopped sweeping and looked up at Nina. "I just meant that I need to keep busy. But now that you mention it, I probably should move out, right? I can't live with my dead husband's family forever. I need to get on with my life."

"Not until the baby is born, though," Nina said.

"Why not?" Izzy asked. "If I'm going to be a single mother, anyway? What am I waiting for? All I do is cook and clean for them anyway. I mean, I love the Morans, don't get me wrong. They've been very good to me. But, once George is born, I'll need to find daycare. Mr. Moran and the boys are not going to help me."

Izzy swept the floor under another station and then stopped again.

"How am I going to do this?" Izzy cried. "How am I supposed to do this all alone? Damn you, Carlos!"

"Come here." Nina embraced Izzy who sobbed on her shoulder.

"What am I going to do?" Izzy kept repeating.

Seventeen

IZZY

WHEN IZZY HAD CALMED DOWN, NINA SAID, "WE HAVE a half-hour before Mrs. Goldman comes in. Why don't you run to Starbucks?"

Izzy wiped her eyes and draped her apron on a chair.

"Do you want anything?" she asked.

"Tall latte, please," Nina said.

At Starbucks, Izzy settled into an upholstered chair, opened the Facebook app on her phone, and started typing.

Izzy: Carlos is dead. Ambush in Afghanistan.

Shawna: OMG. Are you OK?

Luciana: :(

Izzy: I think I'm still in shock. I need to figure out what to do. I'm living with his family. I should move out, right?

Aleecia: You're due this month? You should stay until George is born, though, don't you think?"

Jasmine: Wake up girl! They won't even take George in daycare until he's 2 months old.

Shawna: Where have you been?!

Jasmine: I'm here. I can't get over losing Orchid.

Izzy: I'm so sad for you.

Jasmine: What about you? You lost your husband.

Izzy: Nothing comes close to losing a baby.

Luciana: I'm out. I just had an abortion.

Izzy gasped. She remembered the conversation she overheard between Gilda and Carlos. He'd been worried that she might abort the baby. And now Gilda was dead and Carlos was dead and Luciana's baby was dead and Jasmine's baby was gone. She started to cry. *This is too sad. I'm never going on Facebook again.* She closed the app and texted Pete.

Hi.

Pete texted back, How are you holding up?

Not good, she replied.

Where are you?

At the Starbucks next door to the salon.

Do you want me to come over?

No, that's okay. I'm working.

What time are you done?

I work until 6.

I'll pick you up at 6. We'll go get some pizza?

Okay.

///

Pete's car pulled up outside the salon at five minutes after six.

"Is that Pete's car?" Nina asked. "What's he

doing here? After all the terrible things he said about Carlos?"

"He hasn't said anything bad about Carlos," Izzy said. "Carlos was just a victim of bad policy. Did you know that the French troops he was supposed to be protecting had no idea what they were getting into that day? Just another needless casualty."

"Izzy?" Nina asked incredulously.

"What?" Izzy replied. "Just because I'm educating myself?"

///

Izzy hauled herself into Pete's car, thinking, *this is getting ridiculous. It is time for baby George to vacate the premises!*

"Pizza A-Go-Go?" Pete asked.

"Oh, yeah," Izzy said. "That's the best." She was imagining the smell of sausage, sauce, and onion when her stomach started to heave. It was the strangest sensation, like an earthquake undulating from her pelvic bone to her rib cage. "Oh, God! I think I'm going to be sick!"

"What?" Pete asked. "Right now?"

"Yes," Izzy said. "Right now. Stop the car." She opened the door and leaned out to puke in the gutter.

"Wow," Pete said. "What brought that on?"

"I don't know," said Izzy. She wiped the back of her hand across her lips. "Oh, no! Here we go again!" She leaned out of the car door once more and vomited. When it had passed, she leaned back in her seat with her eyes closed. "I think I need to go to the hospital."

Eighteen

PETE

PETE PULLED THE CAR UP TO THE EMERGENCY room entrance and jumped out. "A little help here!" he cried. "We have a woman in labor!"

Two people in scrubs, a younger man and an older woman, jogged toward the car with a gurney. The young man opened Izzy's door.

Izzy's eyes were rolling back in her head and her body was convulsing.

"She's seizing," the young man said to the woman. The woman called for help and in a flash, six people lifted Izzy from the car and lowered her onto the gurney.

"Are you the father?" the young man shouted to Pete.

"No," Pete said. "The father died in Afghanistan. I'm family, though."

"Park the car and come find us," the female nurse said. They wheeled Izzy into the E.R.

By the time Pete got inside, Izzy was nowhere in sight. He checked in with admissions.

"Are you the father?" the clerk demanded.

"No," Pete said. "He's dead. Afghanistan."

The clerk's tone shifted dramatically. "I'm so sorry for your loss. Are you family?"

"Yes," Pete lied.

"We'll need this paperwork filled out," the clerk said as she handed him a clipboard.

Pete looked over the paperwork. He had no idea what kind of insurance Izzy had, but he knew that with Carlos being in the military, she would have some kind of benefits. Should he have taken her to a military hospital? He realized he couldn't answer any of the questions. He couldn't think of what to do so he called the last home number he had for her.

Dotty answered on the fourth ring. "Hello?" She sounded drunk.

"Mrs. Fiorna?" Pete asked. "This is Peter Grant. Izzy's friend from high school?"

"Who?" Dotty sounded confused.

"Izzy and I were friends in high school," Pete said. "I'm calling because she's in the hospital. Can you come?"

"What is she doing in the hospital?" Dotty asked. "Is she in labor?"

"I don't know," Pete said. "Maybe? She barfed a couple of times, and sort of passed out, and then she might have had a seizure. Can you come?"

"Did you call the Morans?" Dotty asked.

"I don't know their number," Pete said. "Can you call them?"

Pete hung up, pleased with himself for rising to

the occasion and calling in the cavalry. He sat back and waited. He didn't have to wait long. The first to arrive was Mr. Moran.

Pete jumped up and handed the clipboard back to the admissions clerk. "This is Izzy's father-in-law. He can fill out the paperwork for you." Pete slunk back to the far corner of the waiting room.

Mr. Moran was quite agitated with the clerk, demanding to see Izzy right away.

Dotty showed up. Pete found himself hoping she hadn't driven herself to the hospital. She still seemed quite drunk as she badgered the admissions clerk, "Where is my daughter?"

Pete started to feel bad for Izzy. Who would she rather see in her state—the father of her dead husband or her abusive, alcoholic mother? Pete decided then and there: *she would want to see me.*

Pete waited for his moment, then pushed through the double doors leading into the ward. He peered in every room. Finally, he found her. Izzy was hooked up to an IV and there were two nurses buzzing around the room. Izzy looked ter-rified.

"What's happening?" Pete asked as he approached her bed.

One of the nurses spun around. "What are you doing in here?"

"I, I wanted to see how she's doing."

"Well, you have to leave," she hissed. "We're taking her for an emergency C-section." The nurse unlocked the wheels of Izzy's bed with her foot. The other nurse grasped the head of the bed and they began wheeling it out of the room.

"But is she okay? Is the baby okay?"

"Her blood pressure is too high, that's what caused the seizure. We need to get the baby out, now. Now, move!"

Pete jumped away from the doorway just in time. "Izzy!" he called.

"Call my dad," she said, looking pale and afraid. "My phone is in my jacket pocket."

Pete retrieved Izzy's phone and dialed Izzy's

father, Frank. It went to voicemail. "Uh hi, Izzy is in the hospital—SLU Hospital. Having the baby." He hung up.

Pete returned to the waiting room, where he chewed his fingernails nervously for what felt like forever. Mr. Moran and Dotty were sitting there, sipping coffee out of paper cups. Just then, Izzy's dad, Frank walked in.

"Oh, now you show up," Dotty said sarcastically.

Frank ignored her. "What's happening?" he asked.

"They are taking her into surgery for a C-section," Pete said.

"A C-section?" Ricardo cried. "Why? What's happening?"

"I don't know," Pete said. "Something about high blood pressure and they had to get the baby out fast."

"That's Izzy for you," Dotty said, sipping her coffee. "Never a dull moment."

Frank walked over to the window and pulled out his phone. "Hi, honey. She's going in for a C-section," he said into the phone. "I'll be here for a couple of hours."

"Who are you talking to?" Dotty cried out.

What a fucking circus, Pete thought.

Nineteen

IZZY

OVER AN HOUR LATER, DURING WHICH THEY ALL WERE moved to a new section of the hospital, a man named Dr. Bailey came into the waiting room. "Mother and baby are doing fine. George was born at nine-oh-seven p.m. Izzy was having some blood pressure problems that caused her to have seizures. We had to give her some medication to stop them, which worked, but her blood pressure was still dangerously high. She's recovering fine, though, and you should be able to see her soon," Dr. Bailey said. "George came through like a champ, at nine pounds one ounce. A healthy baby. Would you like to see him?"

Ricardo, Dotty, Frank, and Pete all jumped up at the same time.

"One person at a time, okay?"

Pete and Ricardo looked at each other. Neither of them looked at Dotty.

"Why don't you go?" Pete asked Ricardo.

Ricardo followed Dr. Bailey thought the double doors. "He's in the nursery. Follow the blue line on the floor."

Ricardo stood outside the nursery and gazed through the window at his grandson, who was awake and waving his arms and legs. Ricardo pressed both of his hands to the glass and laughed with joy. "Raring to go," he said. "Just like your dad."

Soon, he was joined by Dotty, Frank and Pete.

"Dr. Bailey said Izzy is zonked," Dotty said.

"Give me a call when she's awake," Frank said. "I've got to get back."

"Of course you do," Dotty said. She trailed him down the hall and out the door to the parking lot.

Ricardo and Pete stood at the nursery window, wondering at the miracle before them.

//

Izzy and George stayed in the hospital for three days and Pete visited every day.

"How are you feeling?" Pete asked.

"Honestly, I feel like shit." Izzy said. "I want to poop so bad! These meds make me constipated."

"Do you want to get up and take a walk?" Pete asked. "That's what Nurse Tina recommended. Lots of walks."

"Don't you have class?" Izzy asked.

"Don't worry about me," Pete said. "I've got it covered."

Pete helped her out of bed and with her robe. He held her arm as they walked down the hall and into the next wing.

"I feel stupid," she said. "This is embarrassing, being dressed like this."

"What are you talking about?" Pete said. "It's a hospital. Nobody cares what you're wearing."

They passed by the cafeteria and a gift shop. Izzy found the whole place depressing.

"Where are you going when you get out of here?" Pete asked.

"I'll stay with the Morans for a couple of months," Izzy said. "But then I need to get back to work and I'll find some kind of child care for George."

"What would you think about moving in with me?" Pete asked.

"Are you crazy?" Izzy asked.

"My lease is up and I found a great two-bedroom in Central West End," Pete said. "But, I really can't afford it by myself."

Izzy didn't say anything. The Central West End was the desirable neighborhood for twenty-somethings. She was supposedly getting some money from the military but it hadn't come yet. The Causality Assistance Officer had said something about health care, too, but it was all still a blur.

Did Pete just need her help in paying the rent? she wondered. *Or was he asking for something more? What would people think?*

"I need some time to think about it," she said.

"I already put a deposit down," Pete said with a confident smile. "Are you in?"

Izzy considered her alternatives: a) She could live with the Morans for as long as she liked. In that scenario, she'd be cooking and cleaning for them until she was middle-aged and nobody was going to help her with George, or b) she could move back in with her mom. Well, actually her mom hadn't invited her but she assumed she could force the issue. Now there was option c) move in with Pete, which was weird on so many levels.

"I don't know," Izzy said. "Carlos has only been gone a few weeks. Ricardo needs us right now."

"You're right," Pete said. "Look, I'd better get

back to class. Can you find your way back to your room?" He left Izzy standing in the hallway outside the cafeteria.

"Are you joking?" Izzy yelled at Pete's retreating back. "I'm not supposed to be walking around by myself!"

"You'll be okay, Izzy," he said. "I know how strong you are." He smiled that same unaffected smile.

//

The next morning, Izzy was discharged and Ricardo came to pick them up. He had outfitted the van with a baby seat and he strapped George in.

Ricardo seemed to have aged ten years since Gilda died.

"Ricardo," Izzy said as Ricardo pulled out of the parking lot. "I can't live with you and the boys forever."

"Let's not talk about it right now," Ricardo said. "You need a couple of months to recover. We can talk about it then. I already spoke with the boys. They'll pitch in with the housework."

"I just meant," Izzy continued. "That George and I need to get on with our lives. I should find my own place."

"Yes, yes," Ricardo said. "In a few months. There's no rush. I made up the front bedroom for you and the baby, so you will have your own bathroom."

"Gilda's room?" Izzy asked. She suddenly felt nauseous. *The room where Gilda died?*

"I made it into a nursery," Ricardo said. "It's nice, you'll see."

///

That night, Carlos came to Izzy in a dream. It was the first time she had dreamt about him. He was wearing his fatigues and holding George in his arms. George was fussing and squirming and wouldn't settle down until Izzy took the baby.

Carlos turned to leave the room but he stopped at the door and looked back at her. "Be a good girl," he said.

She woke up in a cold sweat.

"Carlos?" she called out. "Carlos, come back."

She got up and walked over to George's crib. He startled and made fish-like sucking motions with his mouth. Izzy sat on her bed and nursed George until he fell back to sleep. *You look so much like your daddy,* she thought. She didn't want to put him down. "Poor baby," she whispered to her sleeping infant. "You'll never know your daddy. And your daddy was *great*! He would be so proud of you. And he would love you so, so much. But it's just me now and I'm going to be the best mommy ever. I promise." Izzy lay down and cuddled with him until daylight began to peek in through the slats of the blinds.

"What are we going to do, baby?" Izzy whispered. "What are we going to do without your daddy?"

Twenty

IZZY

IZZY HEARD RIC BANGING AROUND IN THE KITCHEN SO SHE
got up, put on her robe, and carried George in
to see what was going on.

"Good morning," Izzy said.

"I made coffee," Ricardo said.

"I dreamt about Carlos last night," Izzy said.

Ricardo looked down at the floor. "I dream
about him every night. I think he was scared."

Izzy started to tear up. "He sounded scared every
time we Skyped," she said. "This is a terrible war.
We need to stop the killing."

"And then what would he have died for?" Ricardo asked.

Izzy kissed George's head. "I will never let my son join the military," she said. "He's going to be a senator." George gazed up at her with his deep brown eyes. "You're going to be a senator, aren't you?"

Ricardo laughed. "A senator? Where did that come from?"

"Somebody once told me, 'George Moran, that's a serious name. He should be a senator.'"

//

"When are you coming back to work?" Nina asked Izzy over coffee. "I know it's only been a few weeks but I need to plan ahead. Should I hire someone temporarily?"

"Here's the problem," Izzy said. "I need someone to look after George." She reached over to George lying in his carriage and wiped the drool off of his chin with a napkin. She poked a finger inside of his diaper to see if he was wet. "I've been doing some research online and saw that Super Scripts has on-site day care. I could take George to work with me. Wouldn't that be great?"

"Yeah, great." Nina didn't sound enthusiastic.

"I figured you had already hired Patty," Izzy said. "I didn't think you needed me anymore."

"I was thinking of expanding and adding a couple of stations," Nina said. "Let me know if you don't get the job."

"Thanks for the vote of confidence!" Izzy said.

"I just miss you," Nina said. "I thought we had a good thing going. I wish there was a way that you could bring George to the salon."

"You have no idea how much work a baby is," Izzy said. "He'd be crying every other minute. I don't think your clients would appreciate it. He might even be bad for business."

"And the Moran's won't help?" Nina asked.

"Are you kidding?" Izzy said. "Ric and the boys, they are helpless."

"What were you and Carlos planning to do?" Nina asked.

"Well we weren't planning on anybody dying, that's for sure," Izzy said.

"I'm sorry about Carlos," Nina said.

"No, I meant Gilda," Izzy said. "We never saw that coming. We thought she'd be there to help out with the baby."

"What about your mom?" Nina asked.

"Are you kidding?" Izzy exclaimed. "Have you heard the stories she tells about me when I was a baby?"

"You mean the one about how you were such a good baby because you slept all day?"

"Right. Slept all day?" Izzy said. "Doesn't that mean I was awake all night?"

"She said she would wheel your crib into the living room, turn on a lamp, wind up your mobile and you would lie there all night, contented and cheerful, watching the little birds go around and around," Nina said.

Izzy pictured that little baby lying alone in the living room night after night with only the colored birds suspended over her crib for company. *Am I imagining it or do I actually remember that mobile playing Rock-a-bye Baby until its spring wound down and then the little birds, pink, blue, yellow and green, floated freely in the ocean breeze that wafted though the open window?* "Exactly! Is that what we want for Baby George? To be neglected all day and then have him keep me up all night?" She rubbed George's tummy. "Isn't that right, baby? Not you, we're not going to let your horrid old Grandma Dots terrorize you."

///

Izzy's job was in the call center at Super Scripts. Her hours were seven to three. She found working in the call center a completely demoralizing and emotionally numbing experience. Her first day "live" on the phones, her headset plugged in like a tether or leash, she kind of lost it. Suddenly, she forgot every single damn thing she had learned in training.

"If you swear at me one more time Mr. Wilson, I will have to terminate this call." She threw off her headset, jabbed a code into the phone so she wouldn't get another call, and strode across the room toward Mr. Firestone, the trainer, as fast as she could without looking like something was wrong.

It was written all over her face. She needed to get the hell out of that room for a few minutes to gather herself. Mr. Firestone didn't hesitate to give her the go-ahead. Almost tripping over herself to get out of the building, practically kicking down the door to the outside world.

Fuck.

Fuck, fuck, fuck, fuck.

At that moment, they were all assholes. Everyone in the whole world was an asshole.

And that was her first day.

Lana sat in the cubicle next to Izzy. She had perfected a sugary sweet, baby-like voice; what she called her "customer service voice." She used that voice on customers in an effort to render them silent and to actually facilitate a productive conversation that might go somewhere. Sometimes it worked, other times it made the customers even angrier. Lana could switch from her regular voice to that customer service voice of hers without missing a beat, or batting an eyelash—even though they were several octaves apart.

The first time Izzy heard it, she thought, *Oh God, how faaaaake*, but very quickly Izzy learned Lana was on to something. She knew what she was doing, she was smart, Izzy thought. They became sisters in arms and to top it off, Lana had a baby in the nursery as well.

The Super Scripts nursery was on the second

floor. The new mothers were given breaks at nine-thirty and two to express breast milk, which was stored in labeled bottles in a refrigerator in the nursery. All of the mothers took their lunch break with their children in the company cafeteria.

Izzy picked up George from the nursery at noon and joined Lana and her baby, Tiffany, for lunch.

"Will you watch Tiff for me, while I grab some food?" Lana asked as she placed Tiffany's carrier on the table. "What can I get you?"

"Soup and salad special," Izzy said. "The usual."

Izzy held George in her lap and rocked Tiffany's carrier with her free hand until Lana came back with a tray of food.

"Did you meet the new sales guy?" Lana asked as she bit into her sandwich.

"He's hot," she mumbled through a mouthful.

"Where?" Izzy asked.

Lana pointed across the room to a table of men and women dressed in suits.

"Which one are you talking about?" Izzy asked.

"The guy sitting next to the blonde," Lana said.

It was Pete! *What was he doing here?* Izzy thought. "I know that guy!" Izzy said. "We went to high school together. But I thought he was in college. What's he doing here?"

Twenty One

IZZY

IZZY KEPT HER EYES ON PETE'S TABLE AS SHE ATE HER salad. When he got up to dump his trash he looked over and saw her. He had a broad smile on his face as he walked toward them

"He's coming over," Lana squealed.

"Pete!" Izzy said. "I didn't know you worked here."

"I just started," Pete said. "How long have you been here?"

"Three months," Izzy said.

"Wow, George is getting big," Pete said. "Hey, George. How are you doing, buddy?"

George gave Pete a big gummy smile.

Pete sat down next to Lana.

"Do you know Lana?" Izzy asked. "We work together in the call center."

"Call center, huh?" Pete said. "How is that?"

"It's a sweat shop," Lana said. "We have a quota, forty calls per hour. They time us down to the second. Time is everything: military clocking-in, monitored toilet breaks, strict call-length control . . . welcome to the world of the robot. Get the customer off the phone in ninety seconds or less. And the customers are such assholes!"

"And I thought we were selling excellent customer service," Pete said laughing.

"You're looking at it," Lana said.

Is Pete flirting with Lana? Izzy wondered. *Why hadn't she heard from him since he left her in the hospital?* The last time she saw him he had asked her to be his roommate. *What was going on with him?*

"What happened to UMSL?" Izzy asked.

"I switched to night school so I could work during the day," Pete said. "I needed more money to make the rent. You should come visit, the neighborhood is great."

"So you two were friends in high school?" Lana asked.

"Not really," Pete said. "I was Carlos's friend. I was at his funeral." Then he paused. "I'm sorry, Izzy. Me and my big mouth."

Izzy blushed. "Don't be. I feel better when people say his name," she said. "Otherwise it's like he never existed."

"But now, we are way more than friends. I was there when George was born, wasn't I, George?" Pete grabbed George's foot and gave it a playful tug.

George giggled.

"Really?" Lana said. "Do tell."

"He drove me to the emergency room," Izzy said. "We were going out for pizza. This was right after Carlos had died. I barfed in his car."

"You haven't seen each other since George was born?" Lana asked.

There was an uncomfortable silence.

"No, we haven't," Izzy said, quietly. "Hey, I think we need to get these babies back to the nursery." She stood to gather George and his things. Lana jumped up too and cleared their trays.

"See you around." Lana waved goodbye to Pete.

Pete looked at Izzy, then he held his hand to his ear and mouthed the words, *call me*.

//

"He wants you to call him," Lana said once they were in the elevator. "What happened between the two of you?"

"I can't figure him out," Izzy said. "We ran into each other while Carlos was away and I thought we were friends. After Carlos died, it seemed like he wanted to be more than friends. He asked me to move in with him. But it was too soon. Carlos's family would never have forgiven me. When I said no, Pete disappeared and I never heard from him again."

"You still live with your in-laws?" Lana asked.

"I've been living with them since we got married," Izzy said. "But it's time for me to move on. They know that."

"If he asked you to move in now, would you do it?" Lana asked.

"No!" Izzy said. "I haven't even seen him in months."

"I don't know," Lana said. "It seems like he likes you. He wants you to call him."

"If he wanted to, he could just call me," Izzy said. *Do I want him to call me? Sure, I would love to go on a date now and then, and yes, he is very attractive. But I can't get over the way he left me in the hospital. And I haven't heard from him since. I'm just not sure how to read him.*

The elevator door opened on the second floor and the girls took the babies back to the nursery. The day-care worker reached for George but he buried his face Izzy's shoulder and clung to her. She didn't want to let him go either but she knew Mr. Firestone would dock her pay if she was late to return from lunch.

"It's okay, baby," Izzy cooed. "Sharon loves you, right Sharon? Don't worry, George, I'll pick you up at three on the dot."

Izzy dabbed her eyes as she caught up with Lana at the elevator.

As the elevator door closed, Lana said, "So, I just got a really random piece of news. My roommate is moving out."

"Really?" Izzy perked up.

Lana smiled, "Yeah, so I don't know, do you want to move in with us?"

"Wait, where is Tiffany's daddy?" Izzy asked.

"Gary comes and goes," Lana said. "He's never

lived with us. Bring George over after work and check out my place."

//

Izzy followed Lana's car to her home that afternoon. She lived in a four-story brick apartment complex that was shaped like a U, the buildings separated by a grassy courtyard where kids were kicking a soccer ball. There was a mangy-looking dog tied to a tree.

Lana lived on the second floor near the stairwell. Her roommate hadn't quite moved out. The place was littered with half-packed boxes and piles of clothes.

"This is nice!" Izzy exclaimed. *Kind of dark, the windows are a little small but the bedroom is a pretty good size. My stuff will fit in here. And George's crib.* "You know I have a cat, right?"

"As long as you keep the litter box in your room, I'm cool," Lana said.

Over dinner, Izzy broached the subject.

"Dad, I'm thinking about moving out at the end of the month," Izzy said.

Oscar and Willie stopped eating.

"What about Mr. Pickles?" Willie asked. Willie was scratching Mr. Pickles' neck under the table and feeding him scraps of food from his plate.

"Mr. Pickles is coming with me, silly," Izzy said. "I found an apartment with a girl from work. She has a little girl about George's age. And the building is pet-friendly."

"What about the van?" Oscar asked. "Can I have the van?"

"The van belongs to Izzy," Ricardo said, sternly. He looked at Izzy with sad eyes. "You'll come back to visit?"

"Of course, I will. How about Sunday dinner?"

Izzy suggested. "What if I came over and made dinner on Sundays?"

"That would be very nice," Ricardo said.

"That would be awesome!" Willie said. "Will you bring Mr. Pickles?"

"Yes, I'll bring Mr. Pickles." Izzy laughed.

Twenty Two

IZZY

LANA HAD LIED. GARY WAS OVER AT THE APARTMENT TWO TO three times a week. He would come in late, after Izzy was in bed, and leave before dawn. Izzy tossed and turned as they made noisy love in the next room. *How can Tiffany sleep through that?* she wondered.

"So I'm guessing I know why your roommate moved out," Izzy said to Lana one morning.

"Did we wake you?" Lana asked. "I'm sorry."

"Is he married?" Izzy asked. "Is that why he doesn't live with you? Where does he go at two o'clock in the morning?"

"He says he lives with his mother," Lana said. "And he's a contractor so he starts work at five a.m."

"But, then why leave at two a.m. if he doesn't have to start work until five?" Izzy pressed. "Doesn't that story sound just a little fishy to you?"

"I guess . . . " Lana sounded unsure.

"If he won't live with you, why doesn't he at least help with the rent so you don't need a roommate," Izzy asked.

"I like having a roommate," Lana said. "Especially now that George is here. You never complain when Tiffany is fussy. My old roommate bitched all the time. And besides, now we can share the parenting."

Share the parenting? Izzy thought. *I didn't sign on for that. Am I expected to babysit Tiffany?*

"I mean like, if you're running late," Lana said. "I can get George ready in the morning. Or vice versa."

Izzy thought about it. *Well that doesn't sound too*

bad. That might actually be a big help. "Speaking of which," Izzy said. "We're both going to be late if we don't get moving."

//

Izzy dropped George at the nursery and after kissing him goodbye, dragged herself back down to her cubicle where she slouched down into her swivel chair, set the pneumatic adjustment to the lowest height, and, craning her neck, closed her eyes to slits. She played with a paper clip she had found on the floor, her fingers warping and bending it.

At this point nothing about humanity could surprise her. Every time a new call came in, she braced herself for hysterical hatred and ugliness.

The caller was repeating his account code.

"Is that Q for Quebec?" Izzy asked.

"No, Q for cube," the customer replied. "N for envelope."

Give. Me. Strength. Fair enough, not everyone

needs to know the military-like phonetics that form a call-center worker's language, but, c'mon, 'N' for envelope? I fear for your children, Izzy fumed.

In moments like those she was grateful for Lana's companionship. Between calls, they shared cynical laughter, smirks, tears of frustration and eye-locked silence that meant more than words could convey. They had developed a strong bond over things that could have broken them individually had they not had each other. Izzy loved mouthing *I'm dying* to Lana and seeing her despairing reply, *Me too!* Knowing someone else was suffering the same fate as her made getting through each eight-hour shift a lot less daunting for Izzy. *If we die, we die together.*

At least once every hour, her screen would freeze and she was forced to engage in the dullest small talk imaginable.

"What's the weather like where you are?" the customer would ask and Izzy wanted to reply, *I don't know, I'm in an industrial box of cubes, drowning in artificial light and the glare of computers. Tell me more about this alien world "outside" of which you speak.*

And there was the daily call from a lonely widow; the call would wreak havoc on her monthly stats. When that dear old lady on the other end started telling Izzy about her boiler, or her next-door neighbor's granddaughter's dog and how hard all these passwords were nowadays, Izzy knew she was *not* hanging up anytime soon. She looked at the timer on her screen. *The call time is already at thirty-six minutes; will this agony ever end?*

There was nothing more satisfying to Izzy than "accidentally" releasing a call from a customer who she had been on for at least a half-hour, in which he personally called her every swear word under the sun and questioned her ability at the job. *Oops, I dropped the call. Sorry about that!* Unless when he called back, she was the person that got the call. No fun, no fun at all.

The worst were the calls that came in at two fifty-nine.

"Happy to help, Mr. Customer," Izzy said in the most rushed, desperate, and minimalist way possible. *Please hang up and get on with your life so I can be released from this prison,* she thought. Oh, and guess what? Of course he didn't know his account number and had to plough through every room of his house to find it. Or she was a first-time customer that absolutely needed to hear the *entire* terms and conditions recited to her—just when she had to pick up George by five minutes after three o'clock or else pay for an extra hour of childcare!

On those days, Izzy would just wave slowly and open-mouth cry as she watched Lana discard her headset and skip away from the office.

//

"Lana," Izzy said when she finally arrived home at four o'clock. "About that co-parenting idea? Do you think you could check George out of the nursery when you know I'm stuck on a call? I'd do the same for you."

"What would I do with George?" Lana asked.

"I'll meet you in the lobby or the parking lot," Izzy said. "Whatever. Just save me the twenty bucks of overtime."

"Okay," Lana said, reluctantly. "We'll probably have to fill out some extra paperwork with the nursery."

"Fine," Izzy said, exasperated. "So we'll fill out some fucking paperwork."

"Bad day?" Lana asked.

"Is there such thing as a good day?" Izzy asked. "How many swear words did you hear today?"

Lana switched into her Customer Service voice. "Oh, I do declare, that's a new word to me!" She switched back to her Lana voice. "I try to shock them into thinking that they've injured my delicate sensibilities."

"How long have you been doing this?" Izzy asked.

"Ever since high school," Lana replied. "I also did a stint as a phone sex operator. I had a whole different voice for that job. Gary made me stop when I got pregnant—it was freaking him out."

"I can imagine!" Izzy said. "You know, I've been thinking. Nina pings me every other week about coming back to work for her and that hair salon gig is looking better and better. I was almost done with my certification—I only needed a few more hours to be a full-on stylist. The hours and the day care are the only things keeping me hanging on at Super Scripts."

Izzy imagined this scenario and smiled. She was actually starting to see a way out of her current situation. The day before, she had finally gotten the nerve to call the Casualty Assistance Officer. And it turned out that she and George would get to keep their military-sponsored health care. *And* she was getting a hundred thousand dollars! But she had already planned to save most of it for George. She had also learned that there might be some financial help from the military for her to finish her certification. The officer said he was going to find out and get back to her. So she could hopefully be done with Super Scripts soon.

"Do you believe today I actually stabbed myself with a broken paper clip? I poked it into the palm of my hand, over and over, leaving tiny little pin-prick marks. I don't even know why I was doing it. Some kind of bizarre crazed comfort."

"Don't lose it," Lana said. "Do you want a glass of wine?"

"No, I don't want to start drinking," Izzy said. "Did I ever tell you that my mom is an alcoholic?"

"Oh, sorry," Lana said.

"What a fucking mess," Izzy said. "I don't want to end up like her. I need to find another outlet. Kick-boxing or something."

Just then Izzy's phone buzzed. "What the F?" she said. "It's Pete. What does he want?"

"You need to go have some fun," Lana said. "You should see him tonight. I'll watch George.

Gary is coming over for dinner at seven. We are in for the night."

"What?" Izzy asked. "Is his wife out of town?"

"Shut up!" Lana said, laughing.

Izzy picked up the call, "Hello?"

"Hey, it's Pete," he said. "How come you never called me?"

Twenty Three

IZZY

DATING PETE WAS EXCITING, IZZY HAD TO ADMIT. THERE was something a little bit dangerous about him. His moods were erratic and unpredictable. One day he would take her for a long walk by the river and talk non-stop about religion, philosophy, and Middle Eastern politics. The next day, he might push her against a wall and kiss her roughly. She never knew who would come to the door— Dr. Jekyll or Mr. Hyde.

Pete was a rising star within the Super Scripts sales force and he had traded in his car for a fire-engine red BMW convertible. Izzy wasn't sure if he was still going to school at night. When she asked him, he was always evasive in his answers. But she didn't really care. She was tired of being a good girl for Carlos and his family. She found herself regretting her decision to marry so young, though if she hadn't married Carlos she wouldn't have health care or the money from the military. And she wouldn't have George. Either way, she was now a widow and a single mother at nineteen. *Life sucks!* Her mother's words rang in her head: *You should stay single and keep your options open.* She was still young and she wanted to have fun. *Pete sure is fun, lots of fun!*

On the nights that Gary was coming over, Lana would watch George and Pete would pick Izzy up and take her back to his house.

"Please slow down," Izzy cried. "You are driving too fast. I don't want to die and leave George an orphan."

But Pete just laughed and stepped on the gas.

Did he enjoy scaring her? She tilted her head back and watched the sky to avoid looking at the oncoming traffic. *I have to admit, I love this feeling—the wind blowing through my hair.* Although it always looked like a fright wig when they arrived at their destination.

At his house, Pete mixed vodka tonics for himself but Izzy always refused.

"Why are you such a good girl?" Pete teased.

"You've met my mom," Izzy said. "Enough said."

After a couple of drinks, Pete started kissing Izzy and pawing at her blouse.

She loved his physicality. She had never really had that with Carlos. Carlos had always treated her like a princess—like she was fragile, made of china. Pete treated her like the sexual being she was. She enjoyed it when Pete stripped down to his underwear and paraded around the apartment in his Jockey string bikini underwear.

He dimmed the lights and turned down the bed.

"Be my good girl," Pete said. "Take off your clothes and sit on my chest."

Sometimes they would have sex and Pete would come right away and then roll off of her and start to snore. Those nights, she would lie in his bed and stare at the ceiling. Then when she was sure he was asleep she would masturbate under the covers. But, most nights, Pete just wanted to play with Izzy's breasts and have her touch herself. He wouldn't let her touch him and he wouldn't take off his underwear.

"Do you think you might be gay?" Izzy asked.

Pete just gave her a bemused look.

At midnight, the alarm on her phone went off.

"The witching hour," Pete said. He always said the same thing. Izzy dressed hurriedly and Pete drove her back home.

"Why can't you ever sleep over?" Pete asked on the drive home.

"You know I have to bathe and feed George in the morning before work," Izzy said.

"It's Friday," Pete said. "You're not working tomorrow."

"Baby still needs a bath and breakfast," Izzy said. "No days off for mommy."

"Why don't you move in with me?" Pete asked.

"We've had this conversation a hundred times," Izzy said.

"How many times will it take to convince you?" Pete asked.

///

When Izzy walked into her apartment, she knew immediately that something was terribly wrong. Both George and Tiffany were screaming at the top of their lungs.

"Lana!" Izzy yelled. "Where are you?"

Lana had pushed Tiffany's crib into Izzy's room and closed the door. Izzy rushed in and picked up George, trying to comfort him. "You're wet!" she said, disgusted. "Where the hell is Lana?"

Izzy changed both babies and gave them bottles. Once they were settled and suckling contentedly, she went to Lana's room and tried the knob. It was locked. She pounded on the door.

"Lana, are you okay?"

There was no response.

She dialed Pete.

"Miss me already?" Pete asked.

"Can you come back right away?" Izzy asked. "I think something terrible has happened."

"What is it?" Pete asked.

"I can't find Lana and her door is locked," Izzy said.

"I'll be right there," Pete said.

While she was waiting for Pete, Izzy searched the apartment for a tool kit. She found a screwdriver and a hammer in the junk drawer in the kitchen. She was attempting to remove the hinges on Lana's bedroom door when Pete walked in.

"Let me do that," Pete said. "What do you think we'll find in here?"

"I have no idea," Izzy said. "I hope they aren't dead."

With three quick whacks, the hinges were off. Pete tugged at the door to remove it from the frame. They peered into the dark room and Izzy fumbled for the light switch.

The overhead light illuminated Lana and Gary, passed out, naked on the bed. Izzy felt for a pulse and Gary started to snore.

"Drunk!" Izzy said. She was disgusted. "That's it, I'm never leaving my baby with you people again!"

Gary's phone was on the floor and was buzzing. Izzy picked it up; there was a text from someone named Suzy. Where are you, cocksucker? Get your cheating ass home.

"Oh geez," Izzy said. "He *is* married. Lana, what have you gone and done? What should I do?" she asked Pete. "Should I text her back?"

"Drop the phone," Pete said. "Let's not get involved."

They turned off all the lights and climbed into Izzy's bed.

"That's settled then," Pete said. "You're moving in with me tomorrow."

//

When they woke up, the babies were still sleeping and Lana was in the kitchen making pancakes.

"Where's Gary?" Izzy asked. Pete sat down at the table next to her.

"He's gone home to his wife, I guess," Lana said.

"So you knew he was married?" Izzy said.

"He was separated when I met him," Lana said. "I think he moved back in around the time Tiff was born. He said it would hurry the divorce along, but his strategy doesn't seem to be working."

"You think?" Pete asked.

"What happened last night?" Izzy asked.

"You mean the bedroom door?" Lana said. "I have no idea!"

"I mean the babies!" Izzy shouted. "When I got home they were both screaming bloody murder. They were wet and hungry. We took off your door because we thought you had died! We expected to find dead bodies in there. Good thing we didn't call the cops. They would have taken the kids away."

"Gary brought some Oxy over last night," Lana said. "I guess it knocked me out. You know me, I would never neglect the babies."

"Look, Lana," Izzy said. "Pete has asked me to move in with him and that's what I'm going to do."

"What? When?" Lana cried. "I thought we had a good thing going here."

"Today," Pete said.

"Today," Izzy repeated.

Twenty Four

IZZY

PETE PAID FOR THE MOVERS TO PACK AND MOVE IZZY'S stuff to his place. While the movers went about their business, she sat on a blanket on the living room floor playing with George. He was crawling and was starting to try to pull himself up. She felt really good about the decision to move in with Pete. *I will have more time for George instead of having to do all the chores that always seemed to be waiting for me.* Pete had a housekeeper that came in twice a week and he ordered all of his meals from a gourmet chef service. *No more cooking and cleaning!* She bounced George up and down on her knees. He squealed with delight.

//

Izzy quickly fell into her new routine. She got up at five to shower and dress and then woke George up at five-thirty to nurse and bathe. He was eating some solid foods as well. They were out the door by six-fifteen to make sure she had time to get George settled in the nursery before she had to clock in at seven.

She always tried to pick up George on time and arrive home by three forty-five. Pete's apartment was next to a park with a pool and Izzy took George over there every afternoon. He loved the water and was a strong kicker. Pete didn't get home until seven and sometimes later if he had a client event to attend. Izzy loved her one-on-one time with George and he seemed to be thriving.

One evening, returning from a baby Gymboree class with George, Izzy entered the apartment at seven-thirty. As soon as she turned her key in the lock, the door swung open. Pete stood there, his face red and swollen with rage.

"Where the fuck have you been?" Pete demanded. "I expected you to be here for dinner. The food is on the counter, getting cold."

"I'm sorry, I didn't know what time you'd be coming home," Izzy said. "We just got back from Gymboree. I'll put it on the kitchen calendar so you know what days we have class until seven."

"You'll put it on the kitchen calendar?" Pete screamed. "On the fucking calendar?"

"What's wrong?" Izzy asked.

"Are you suggesting that there is something wrong with me?" Pete screamed. "Is it too much to ask that you are here when I get home?"

"You never tell me what time you're getting home," Izzy said in a calm voice. "If you tell me what time, I promise I'll be here."

She walked very cautiously around him, giving him a wide berth as she headed toward George's room. She didn't see the swing coming. He caught her on the back of her head and knocked her to her knees. She clung to George, and held his head close to her chest as she tried to block her fall with her elbows. George's head landed softly on the carpet and he started to wail.

"George!" Izzy cried.

Izzy couldn't get up; the pain in her knees was so intense she thought she must have shattered both kneecaps. She scooted backwards on her butt to rest against the sofa and tried to comfort George even as the pain blinded her.

Pete stormed out of the apartment, slamming the door behind him.

Izzy cuddled George until he calmed down. He wasn't injured; he was just scared.

What the fuck was that? Izzy wondered.

///

That night, Izzy lay in bed, sleeplessly wondering when Pete would come back and what he would do next. He finally came in around midnight, slipped out of his clothes and climbed into bed next to her.

"Are you awake?" Pete asked.

"Yes," Izzy replied.

"Baby, I'm so sorry," Pete said. "I've got this blood sugar thing. I guess I was just hungry and my blood sugar crashed. I didn't know what I was doing; I swear. My old man—he had this problem too. Every now and then he'd knock my mom upside the head—until she finally left him. Please don't leave me. I promise it will never happen again."

Izzy was silent for a long time. She didn't know what to say.

"Okay, baby?" Pete asked. "I love you. Please forgive me and I promise this will never happen again."

Izzy wanted to believe him. After all, she didn't

really have any place else to go. Moving back in with Lana wasn't really an option and she'd enjoyed living in Pete's luxury apartment with all the amenities.

"Okay," she said.

"I love you," Pete said.

"I love you, too," she said. It was a mechanical response. She wasn't at all sure what she felt, except fear.

"That's my girl," Pete said. He pulled her to him and she felt his erection. They made love but this time it was different. He was tender and gentle with her, almost like Carlos used to be. *You do love me*, she thought. He had a blood sugar issue. That's all it was. She just needed to make sure that dinner was ready when he walked in the door.

///

In the morning, Izzy ran through her normal routine. Pete was in the shower when she headed out at six-fifteen. That evening, she made sure that George was in bed and the table was set before the food order arrived. Pete walked in around seven-fifteen and he seemed tense. He approached Izzy to kiss her and she flinched.

"Did something happen at work today?" she asked.

"Just the usual bullshit," Pete said. "I have an account up for renewal and they are leaning toward going with the competition. Too many complaints about our call center."

Izzy startled. "Really?"

"Got your attention, didn't I?" Pete asked. "No—just kidding! They are just negotiating on price. Apparently, CVS is giving away the service."

Pete kissed her hands. "Are we okay?" he asked.

Izzy nodded, reluctantly.

"Let's sit down and have a nice dinner," Pete said. "Is the food still hot?"

"Yes," Izzy said. "The food just got here—I'm keeping it warm in the oven."

The next few weeks went by without incident and Izzy was starting to believe that it was a one-time thing. Until it happened again.

George was in bed and Izzy and Pete were seated at the table enjoying a delicious Indian meal of Chicken Tikka Masala, basmati rice, and onion naan.

"George had a nice day, today," Izzy was saying. "He made a new friend in the nursery, a little girl named Claire. They played very nicely and then Claire's mom and I had lunch together with the kids. We're going to try to get together on the weekend for a play date."

Izzy didn't see the glass coming. She just heard the impact of glass on glass as the wine glass that Pete had hurled at her face missed by a whisker and hit the framed print hanging on the wall behind her.

"Why is it always about your fucking day? Your lunch dates and bullshit!" Pete screamed. "What about my day? And why are you making plans for the weekend without consulting me? Who do you think you are anyway?"

Izzy sat very still.

"Are you satisfied?" Pete hollered. "Now look what you made me do! That print was expensive."

Watching for any sudden movements from Pete out of the corner of her eye, Izzy turned slowly in her chair to look at the print. The impact had shattered the protective glass and several shards were sticking out of the artwork. The red wine was spreading like oozing blood onto the beige carpet.

Izzy got up and walked to the kitchen to get some salt and soda water. As she bent over the stain, Pete approached her from behind. She ducked her head in anticipation of the blow. But instead, Pete gently lifted her to her feet.

"Don't worry about it," he said. "The maid will get it tomorrow."

"The carpet will be ruined by tomorrow," Izzy protested.

"So we'll buy a new carpet," Pete said. "Come to bed; I want to make love to you."

Izzy did as she was told.

Twenty Five

IZZY

IZZY BECAME INCREASINGLY WORRIED FOR HER SAFETY AS well as George's. She never knew what kind of mood Pete would be in when he walked through the door at night. She never knew what would set him off and she wondered how far his anger might carry him.

George was playing, noisily, in the living room and Izzy was wiping down the high chair, when she heard his key in the door. George fell silent and Izzy held her breath. *What kind of mood is he in tonight? Will he kick the closet door off of its hinges? Will he throw dishes? Or will he bypass us altogether and barricade himself in the bedroom to read all night?*

The front door slammed. Pete was in the room.

He was in a jovial mood as he asked, "Did you see the news?"

"What?"

"Jerry Harvey killed his wife and shot himself."

Izzy felt the muscles in her back contract.

"Jerry Harvey, the guy in finance? Do you know who I'm talking about?"

Izzy didn't know what to say. *Yes?*

"The funny thing is, I could see myself doing that, you know?" Pete said.

Did he just say that he could see himself killing me and George? Izzy was terrified and glanced around the apartment for possible weapons. She glanced at the kitchen knives hanging in the rack next to the stove. She tried to position her body between Pete and the knives, hoping to distract him. She knew that she needed to say something but she was afraid that whatever she said might set him off and give him the opening he sought to release his anger.

"That is funny," Izzy said at last.

Pete seemed satisfied with her answer. "What's for dinner?"

"Tonight, we're having Mexican," Izzy said.

"Tequila!" Pete said. "Did you buy Tequila?"

"Yes," Izzy said. "It's in the freezer. The Margarita mix is in the fridge."

Pete gorged himself on fish tacos and margaritas and then he passed out on the sofa, snoring loudly.

///

Izzy started to plot her escape. She had to find a place to live but most importantly, she didn't want Pete to know that she was planning to leave and once she was gone she had to make sure he wouldn't be able to track her down. *Well, that is stupid. He can find me at work. He could stalk me in the parking lot. He could corner me in an elevator and beat me to death.* The more she imagined possible scenarios for her demise, the more panicked she became.

She knew she couldn't live alone; she needed to have a buffer between her and Pete. She considered the alternatives. She could move back in with the Morans—Pete would never mess with Ricardo and the boys. But she would be cooking and cleaning for the Morans every day for the next eighteen years. She didn't want to live life as a celibate widow. That just seemed so bleak. She could move back in with Lana, but Pete wasn't afraid of Lana—or Gary, for that matter. She could ask her mom if she could move back in. *Nobody fucks with Dotty!* That was a real possibility—assuming Dotty would go for it. But Izzy hated the idea of subjecting George to that toxic environment. It wouldn't be long before he started picking up on Dotty's curse words and general hostility. She wanted George to stay pure and innocent for as long as possible. She had her money from the military—but she'd sworn to keep it for George. That left Nina. It made her sick to think that Pete might show up and threaten Nina. It wasn't fair. Nina didn't deserve that.

"Nina," Izzy said into the phone. "Got time to meet for coffee tomorrow?"

//

"Here's the thing," Izzy said. "I'm afraid of Pete. George is afraid of Pete. Shit, even Mr. Pickles is afraid of Pete. I need to get away from him before something terrible happens."

"Did he hit you?" Nina asked. "Because if that fucker hit you, he has me to answer to!"

Izzy lowered her eyes. She felt so ashamed. "Yes," she said in a whisper.

"That's it," Nina declared. "You're out of there!"

"He can't know that I'm planning to leave," Izzy said. "We need to be gone when he gets home from work."

"Good plan," Nina said. "Here's what you'll do. Call in sick and have the movers come during the day while he's at work. When he gets home, you'll be gone."

//

Izzy scheduled the movers to arrive at ten a.m. the following Monday. *Pete will have left for work by then.* She surveyed the apartment. Izzy didn't own much—just a couple of boxes of photo albums and journals and her clothes. Pete had made Izzy toss everything else when she moved in with him. Everything she had owned seemed to offend his sensibility, his sense of style. *In fact, George owns more shit than I do: his crib, bassinet, stroller, playpen, toys, books and clothes. And then there is Mr. Pickles' carrier, litter box, and food bowls.*

But on Friday, Pete showed up unexpectedly at her cubicle.

Izzy was on a call. "Hello, how are you and how can I help you?" she said into her headset. She raised a finger at Pete and mouthed, *give me a minute.*

Pete paced back and forth behind her chair, which made Izzy nervous. She had to ask the customer to repeat his account number three times and re-enter it three times before the system finally recognized it. At last, the call ended and the customer hadn't even cursed at her. She swiveled in her chair to face Pete. She hoped that she wore a warm and welcoming smile on her face.

"Are you moving out?" Pete demanded.

Izzy's smile faded. *How did he find out?* "What?" she asked. "What are you talking about?" All she could think about was rescuing Mr. Pickles. He was still at the apartment. Everything else—clothes, all of George's stuff—she could replace.

But Mr. Pickles—I can't leave him there. I need to retrieve him.

"After you left this morning," Pete said. "A guy came by to drop off boxes."

Fuck! Izzy hadn't thought about that. "Boxes?" she asked.

"Don't play dumb with me," Pete said. "You're leaving me, aren't you?" He spun on his heel and stomped away.

Izzy started freaking out and at the same time, she saw Mr. Firestone giving her the evil eye from across the room. She made a show of adjusting her headset and dialed Nina on her cell.

"Nina!" Izzy whispered into the phone. "He knows I'm leaving. I'm afraid to go home tonight but I need to rescue Mr. Pickles."

"He gets home later than you, doesn't he?" Nina asked. "I'll meet you at your place at four just to be safe."

"What about George?" Izzy asked. "I need him to be safe."

"Ask Lana?" Nina suggested. "Maybe she can watch him tonight?"

Izzy hung up and poked Lana in the arm. "Hey, girl," she said. "I need a favor."

Lana looked at Izzy, coldly. "Are you speaking to me again?" she asked.

"Please don't be like that," Izzy said. "I really need your help. Pete is really scaring me. I need to get away from him—I'm moving in with Nina. I need to go over there after work and rescue Mr. Pickles and I don't want George to be caught in the crossfire. Can you please, please, please take George home with you? I'll pick him up by eight. I promise."

"So you trust me to watch your baby?" Lana asked. Her eyes were dead.

"I'm sorry if I hurt your feelings," Izzy said. "You're a wonderful mom to Tiff. I never meant to imply otherwise. I'm scared and I'm desperate and I really need a friend right now."

Lana's face softened. "You know I love Georgie,"

she said. "I'd never let that prick hurt him. I always told you that Pete was bad news."

Seriously? You did not! Izzy thought. *But this is not the time to bicker.* "Thank you, thank you, thank you," Izzy said. "I owe you. Anytime. Seriously."

Twenty Six

IZZY

ONCE Izzy HAD CONFIRMATION THAT LANA HAD PICKED up George from day care, she steeled herself for the confrontation at home. She drove home slowly and tried to steady her breathing. But as she pulled into the parking lot behind the apartment, she saw Pete's car parked in its space. *Shit! He is waiting for me!*

Nina pulled in behind Izzy and got out of her car.

"His car is here," Izzy said. "He came home early. What am I going to do?" Izzy was shaking and clawing at her arms.

"Calm down. I'm here for you," Nina said. "He can't hurt you as long as I'm here."

Together they entered the apartment. Pete was standing in the living room.

"What is she doing here?" he demanded.

"I'm just here to support Izzy," Nina said.

"Where's George?" Pete demanded.

"He's having a play date with Tiffany," Izzy said.

"You left him with that cunt, Lana?" Pete demanded. "What kind of a mother are you?" Pete advanced on Izzy menacingly and Nina stepped in front of her.

"If you want to hit somebody, asshole," Nina said, "hit me."

"What's your problem?" Pete turned his venom on Nina. "You are so pathetic! You're single and alone and you will never have children. You are jealous of Izzy, aren't you? You wish you had a boyfriend who drove a BMW and lived in a nice apartment, don't you? You feel like you need to come over here to fuck with us? You fucking loser. You piece of shit."

Izzy was stung by his words. She was mortified that she had dragged Nina into this.

"You know who's a loser? Guys that hit women," Nina said. "You can say hateful things but your words mean nothing to me. Izzy asked me to come here and help her collect her things—and her cat. So get the fuck out of our way."

"The cat?" Pete said. "You think that fucking cat is still alive? I drowned it in the toilet and I enjoyed watching him squirm and fight for every breath. I HATED that cat!"

"Mr. Pickles!" Izzy screamed. She pressed her hands to her face in dismay.

Just then, Mr. Pickles wandered out from the hall closet where he had been hiding. Izzy scooped him up in her arms. He moaned in protest.

"Yeah, well I would have killed him if I'd seen him," Pete said.

"Grab his carrier," Izzy said to Nina. "In the closet."

Nina retrieved the carrier and Izzy stuffed Mr. Pickles into it as he meowed loudly.

"Take him outside, please," she said to Nina.

After Nina had left with Mr. Pickles, Izzy was no longer afraid. She turned to face Pete.

"I need to take George's stuff, his crib and some clothes," she said.

"Take whatever you want," Pete said. "I no longer give a shit."

Nina returned and together the two girls gathered what they could. They filled George's crib with his clothes, toys and books. Nina gathered Mr. Pickles' stuff—his litter box and food—and carted it out to her car.

Izzy started emptying the contents of her dresser and piled in on the bed. Pete stood guard in the doorway.

"I'm not going to steal anything of yours," she said.

"Who do you think you are?" Pete asked.

Izzy didn't know what he wanted from her, so didn't answer as she tackled the clothes in her closet.

"Answer me, bitch!" Pete demanded.

Izzy turned to face him. She was shaking. His face was contorted in pain. "I don't know what you want me to say, Pete. I don't feel safe here. I'm worried about George's safety. Your blood sugar . . ."

He cut her off. "You think you can just walk out on me without saying a word? Safe? You don't feel safe? You mooched off me for months, ate my food, cluttered my apartment with your baby shit, and your fucking cat. You are a leech. A fucking parasite!"

"Then I guess you're glad I'm leaving?" As soon as the words left her mouth, Izzy knew she had made a mistake. Pete lunged at her and grabbed her by her hair. He threw her down on the floor in between the bed and the dresser and started to unzip his shorts.

Izzy kicked at him and scooted toward the wall. She snatched the portable phone from the nightstand but he reached behind her and ripped the cord from the wall. She threw the phone at him. He caught it and threw it back at her, and it hit her in the eye. She cried out and clutched her eye. Pete grabbed her legs and tugged her toward him, shoving her skirt up around her waist and ripping off her panties.

"No!" she screamed.

Nina heard the scream and came running. She had already dialed 911 by the time she got to the bedroom and saw clothes scattered everywhere and Pete wrestling with Izzy. She grabbed one of Izzy's shoes and started hitting Pete on the back of his head.

"Get off of her, asshole!" Nina screamed.

Pete roared and lunged at Nina but his shorts were down around his ankles and he tripped and fell headfirst onto the bedpost. The impact stunned him and he slumped onto his knees on the floor. He had a gash in his forehead and blood streamed from the wound.

//

Izzy had grabbed her keys and was about to leave with Nina, when the police arrived.

"Officer, it's okay," Izzy said. "We were just leaving."

"Ma'am, did he hit you?"

Izzy's eye was swollen shut. She must have bit her lip because it, too, was swollen and bleeding.

"We need to take a statement," the officer said.

Nina and Izzy sat at the kitchen table.

Pete was handcuffed. The officer marched him into the living room.

"Do you want to tell us what happened here?"

//

Izzy couldn't sleep that night. It wasn't just Nina's lumpy futon. She felt like the last two years of her life had been a disaster. If she could rewind the clock, she asked herself: *would I have married*

*Carlos, had George, taken the job at Super Scripts
and moved in with Pete? Dear God, please give me a
do-over. I want to get it right this time.*

It came to her in a flash. Her mistake was
taking the job at Super Scripts. Yes, the day care
benefit was awesome but surely she could have
figured out day care on her own if she had just
tried a little harder. It dawned on her—*the need to
find childcare can make you do desperate things.* She
contemplated the next eighteen years of her life.
She feared that there could be many hard times,
many lean times ahead.

The next day, Izzy gave notice at Super Scripts.
She decided not to file charges against Pete but she
did file a restraining order. She never wanted to see
him again. She asked Oscar to make arrangements
with Pete to meet the movers and pack up all her
stuff and deliver it to Nina's place. Izzy was proud
of her newfound confidence and resourcefulness.
Some day, George is going to think I'm awesome!

"I've never been happier sweeping up hair clippings," Izzy said.

"You'll have your license soon," Nina said.

It was true. The Casualty Assistance Officer had called with good news about financial support for her coursework. So, marrying Carlos *had* been the right thing to do; even though he was gone he was still taking care of them. After all, she had George. And that was the greatest thing in her life.

"Maybe you want to get into manicuring as well," Nina added. "There's big bucks in that."

"I'm serious," Izzy said. "You saved my life. I'm so grateful that you rescued me from Pete. I asked God for a do-over and you showed up. You've always been there for me. Thank you." Izzy started to tear up.

"Are you fucking kidding me?" Nina said. "You are family." Nina gave Izzy a big hug. "And you found someone to watch George?"

"There's a lady down the street who offers day care," Izzy said. "Miraculously she had an open spot. I admit it smells a little funny in there. We'll have to see how this works out, but he seems happy for now. The most important thing is that I feel confident that I am a good mom and I can make good decisions for my son. We will be okay. At least until he's twelve or thirteen and he starts blaming me for everything." Izzy laughed.